Kitty from the Start

Other Books by Judy Delton

Kitty
from
the
Start

Judy Delton

Houghton Mifflin Company

Boston

Library of Congress Cataloging-in-Publication Data

Delton, Judy.
    Kitty from the start.

    Summary: Kitty moves to a new neighborhood and eventu-
ally makes a successful transition into her new third
grade.
    [1. Catholic schools—Fiction. 2. Schools—Fiction.
3. Moving, Household—Fiction] I. Title.
PZ7.D388Ke 1987   [Fic]   86-21481
ISBN 0-395-42847-5

Printed in the United States of America

FFG 10 9 8 7 6 5

For Amanda, who reads my books first

Contents

Kitty from the Start

1

Kitty's Father's News

Kitty skipped on the way home from school, even though her mother had warned her about how fast the leather soles of her shoes wore out when she did. Kitty's mother worried a lot about money even though they were not really "poor." She said it was because of the Depression. Kitty was born during the Depression. It was a time when many people were out of work, although Kitty's father had never been out of work. He worked for the telephone company, in Minneapolis, but they lived in Saint Paul because that was where all of Kitty's aunts lived.

Kitty was in the third grade at Saint James

school. The nuns talked about a terrible war in Europe, but Europe was a place very far away, across a huge ocean, and Kitty only remembered the war when Sister John Bosco or Father McNeel asked for donations of canned food to send abroad. Every morning, of course, the class prayed for the "hungry and unfortunate victims of the war," but the rest of the time it was hard to remember things that went on outside of Saint Paul. There was homework to think about and the Saint Paul winter carnival. And there were new books of paper dolls at the dime store and her friends to play with.

As Kitty skipped, she remembered the good news she had had at school. It happened right after lunch. Sister John Bosco had a smile on her face (that indicated a change in routine) as she said, "Boys and girls, we are going to choose people to be in the third grade band today." As Sister began to call names, Kitty crossed her fingers for luck. She wanted to be in the band. And she especially wanted to play the bells.

"Mavis," Sister was saying, "you will play the tambourine." Mavis came to the front of the room and took the tambourine that Sister held out to her. Kitty did not want to play the tambourine. There were many tambourine players. All those players had to do was hit the instrument on their knuckles. Anyone could do it.

Sister called some more tambourine players, but Kitty was not among them. Then she said, "Now for the triangles." Kitty did not want to play a triangle. That was even worse than a tambourine. People without any musical talent played triangles — people like Tom Donay, who (Father McNeel said) did not know a triangle from a trombone.

"Tom Donay," Sister said with a smile. Tom walked forward and reached out his hand for the triangle. Sister called some more triangle players. Finally all that was left was someone to play the bells. The light tinkling bells. Only one lucky person was needed for the bells. The bells gave the band the extra trill — and after the harsh clunk of the tambourine and the sharp sound of the triangle, the bells were like frosting on the cake. Everyone wanted to play the bells.

Now Sister was holding up the leather strap with the bells on it. "Kitty," she said, "I think we will have you play the bells in the band." Everyone else moaned lightly — not because they didn't want Kitty to play them, but because they were disappointed not to be chosen themselves.

Kitty walked proudly to the front of the room. By handing the bells to Kitty Sister was expressing confidence in her. There were several bells on the strap, and the player had to silence certain ones by putting a hand around them, and shake the others. You had to pay close attention to know which bells not to ring. If you rang the wrong ones, it could ruin the whole number, because with only one bell ringer there were no others to cover up for you, as there were with the tambourines and the triangles.

It felt good to relive the happy moment in her mind. She was so busy thinking about how good it felt, that she almost did not see a car come around the corner as she skipped, and drew back just in time! Good news could be dangerous! She gave a little shiver and walked carefully the rest of the way, anxious to share the news with her mother.

When she got to her house on Juliet Avenue, she threw open the door and was surprised to see her father in the kitchen. Her father was never home this early. It was only a little after three o'clock.

Her mother and father stopped talking when Kitty came in.

"I have some good news!" said Kitty, putting her books on the kitchen table and falling into a chair, all out of breath.

"Were you skipping again?" Her mother frowned, looking at Kitty's scuffed brown oxfords.

"I'm going to play the *bells* in the band!" said Kitty, ignoring her mother's question.

Her mother looked at her father. They didn't

look happy. "I have some news too," said her father, putting his hand on the top of her head. "We have to move to another house. Someplace closer to Minneapolis, probably. The landlord is selling this house, and it is a good time to move because we need another bedroom, and a place closer to my office."

What did he mean, a good time to move? A good time to move was not just when Kitty was able to play the bells in the band. No time was a good time to move. She had always lived in this house. It was her house. It was her neighborhood. And Saint James was her school. Sister John Bosco (even as strict as she was) was her teacher. And what about her friends? They all lived around here and went to her school. Even the dime stores and movie houses were familiar and belonged to her. Her father was wrong; it was *not* a good time to move.

"I can't move," said Kitty. "This is our house; we belong here."

"It is our landlord's house," said her mother. "It is Mr. Larson's house."

"Can't we buy it from him?" said Kitty.

Her father shook his head. "He wants too much money. He wants three thousand dollars for it."

That was a lot of money. More than Kitty could even imagine. Most things Kitty spent money for cost five cents, like a candy bar. Or a dime, like a book of paper dolls.

"We'll find a good house," said her father. "A bigger house, and a more convenient house. It will be fun looking for one together."

Kitty went into the bedroom and threw herself on her bed. Here she was, only nine years old, and already a crisis had befallen her. To leave everything she knew and loved behind, and go to a strange house and, worse, a strange school (where everyone would stare at her) was shattering. Kitty was used to getting her own way most of the time. In fact, Aunt Jo often said she was "spoiled." The word reminded Kitty of a ripe plum, or a tomato in the icebox that had gone bad. She did not feel spoiled. Even though she was an only child, she knew how to share.

And she was not selfish, goodness knows. If she had a Popsicle she broke it in half, and in school, why, she could not even count all the erasers she gave away. And sheets of paper.

It really didn't seem too much to ask that her family stay in one place, that they not upset her entire life, make her lose friends and miss the band and leave her familiar classroom. Even a spoiled child deserved that. But by suppertime Kitty realized that she could not change things and she was going to have to face a new life. Her father was reading the "for rent" part of the paper and said they would get on the streetcar and look at a few houses even tonight.

Her mother quickly cleared the table and put the dishes and the pork chop pan to soak. She practically never left dishes for later, so tonight was definitely special. She got out coats, and the family went to the streetcar line, her father with the rental list in his pocket.

It seemed to Kitty they rode forever, the tracks humming beneath them, across grassy fields toward the midway area of Saint Paul. Her father rang the bell when he heard the conductor call "Snelling Avenue," and they all got off and began looking for 541. When they came to it, there was a FOR RENT sign in the front yard. The grass was knee-high, and some shingles were missing from the roof. In the back yard was what Kitty recognized as an outhouse, meaning that the house did not have a bathroom!

"A wasted trip," said Kitty's mother. "We surely don't want to live in *that* house."

Kitty's father crossed that ad off in his paper and said, "There's one on Charles Street. Let's walk by that." It was almost dark when they reached Charles Street. Kitty was sure they had all worn down inches of shoe leather by the time they came to the house in the ad. It looked neat and clean, and her father knocked on the door. The man of the house showed them the rooms. The house had all kinds of rooms, even a bedroom upstairs. And a bathroom with a large tub standing on four lion-clawed feet.

"What is the rent?" said Kitty's father.

"Forty dollars a month," the man said.

Her father thanked him, and they left for the streetcar stop.

"That is highway robbery," said Kitty's mother.

"We can't spend half of a month's salary on rent," her father agreed.

Kitty felt a lost and hopeless ache in the pit of her stomach on the long streetcar ride home. She was a child without a home. A foreigner on the wrong side of the city. Almost an orphan. What would happen if they couldn't find a house they could afford? Would the landlord put them out on the street with their furniture? Would they have to live in a house with no bathroom? Her mother and father looked worried. Kitty thought about the mean, selfish landlord and felt very angry at him. Then she remembered that Sister John Bosco told them whenever they felt anger at one of "God's children" (was the landlord one of God's children?) they should pray for him.

Kitty did not feel like praying for him. She tried, but she couldn't force the words. It made sense to pray for sick people, for lame people, for poor people, for hungry people — but not for mean people. Kitty decided to let the landlord fend for himself.

Saint James school looked different to Kitty the next day. It looked like a very nice school that was out of her reach. Yesterday it had been *hers*; today it was something she had lost. She told Sister John Bosco about the move, and Sister said, "The Lord works in strange ways . . ." and put her serge-draped arm around Kitty's shoulder. She told Kitty that something good would come of the move, and that she should pray for help finding a good home.

If the move was the result of the Lord working in strange ways, Kitty made up her mind then and there she would not pray to Him for a new house. She would just have to take her chances with the rental ads in the paper.

Every evening Kitty's father looked for a house. He decided that Kitty and her mother should come to look only after he had found one that was a possibility. So Kitty went to school every day, but she had the feeling that she did not belong there anymore. When anything was planned, Sister said, "Kitty will be moving, so we won't assign anything to her." And when Eleanor planned a birthday party, she said, "Of course, you will be gone by then." As if Kitty was going to vanish from the face of the earth. Or be swallowed up by a monster fish.

And then one day, when Kitty was feeling the most homeless and unwanted, her father came running to meet her after school. "I found the perfect house!" he said. "It has two bedrooms and a large yard. It is near Saint Anthony's school, and next door to a grocery store! We can move in next week!"

"But is the rent too expensive?" said Kitty, who had grown used to the idea of being homeless.

"It is thirty dollars a month!" said her father. "And well worth it!"

That night, curled up in her bed in the house that was no longer hers, Kitty thought about Saint Anthony's. She had never heard of it. Was it big? More than two stories? Who would her teacher be? Was there a band? Would the children snub her? She fell asleep and dreamed that her new teacher asked her, "What is the capital of New Mexico?" and Kitty did not know. She sat down in disgrace and then was called on again. "What is the square root of forty-two?"

"We didn't have square root yet at Saint James," said Kitty in her dream.

After five more questions that Kitty could not answer, she found she was in the wrong classroom!

"This is the fifth grade," said the nun, who, in the dream, looked something like Kitty's grandfather, with an Adolf Hitler–type mustache.

Kitty woke up feeling partly relieved at being in the wrong room and partly embarrassed. Saint

Anthony's grew larger and larger and more and more foreign to her in her mind.

Finally moving day came, the van was packed, Aunt Jo came to help wash cupboards and line shelves, and Kitty left her old life behind forever.

2

The First Day at Saint Anthony's

Kitty's new house was on Jefferson Avenue. Right next door (in fact, with only a lilac hedge between them) was Stenstrom's grocery store. Stenstrom's had a penny candy counter, which was convenient to have so close, and her mother said the store would be handy for shopping. "If we run out of anything, we can run next door in a few moments!" she said.

The house had a fine screened front porch where Kitty's mother put their green rocking chair, and it was fun to sit there cozily with a book and watch the traffic go by. Jefferson was a busier street than Juliet had been.

The neighbors on the other side of Kitty's house were an older couple, Mr. and Mrs. Thone. They seemed to work all day long in their large garden, sometimes leaning on a rake or hoe to watch the furniture moving in next door or Kitty carrying in her collection of dolls.

Kitty loved dolls. She had rubber dolls that wet, and dolls with plaster of Paris heads and soft bodies, and rag dolls that had gone limp with too much love. She had a yellow teddy bear called Bubbles and a pink long-eared rabbit called Bunny Bosco, after Sister John Bosco. Personally, Kitty thought it was a better name for a rabbit than for a nun.

One evening after the furniture was all in place and the boxes were almost unpacked, Kitty's father said, "Let's walk over to Saint Anthony's and take a look at your new school."

Kitty had pictured Saint Anthony's in her mind now for so long, she had almost forgotten that it was a real place. She felt both anxious and afraid at the same time, but she got her coat out of the closet and she and her father started down Jefferson Avenue.

"You walk one block on Jefferson," said her father, "and then turn right at the corner and keep walking along Albert Street until you come to Randolph."

The streets and houses and shops were all so new to Kitty that she wondered if she would remember how to get there on Monday. After what seemed like quite a walk Kitty's father said, "Well, there it is, your new school!"

Saint Anthony's was not what Kitty expected. Her old school, Saint James, was a dark-red brick building dwarfed beside a towering limestone church, but Saint Anthony's stood forlornly on the corner, with a fence around it.

"Where is the church?" said Kitty.

"The church is in the school," said her father. "They will build another church across the street someday, but for now the church is on the main floor of the school."

Kitty had never heard of a church inside of a

school. A church should be *larger* than a school, not fit inside! She stared at Saint Anthony's. It was made of modern light-colored brick and looked a little plain and impersonal to Kitty.

"This is a new neighborhood, you know," said her father, as if reading her thoughts. "There has not been time or money to finish all the building."

Maybe that was what gave the building the appearance that it could disappear overnight, that if Kitty went there the next day there could be only an empty lot with blowing weeds on the spot. Saint James had been old and permanent, and Kitty liked the dependable feeling Saint James had. It would never disappoint her and disappear.

In the back of Saint Anthony's, Kitty noticed some swings and slides and a makeshift teeter-totter.

"Now, you will probably go in that door right there on Monday," said her father, pointing. "You can see what the other children do."

Kitty hated to depend on complete strangers

who did not even know she was coming, to show her what to do. It made her feel unsettled and windblown.

On the way home, Kitty's father again seemed to know what she was thinking, because he said, "Maybe I should go to the office later and take you to the classroom myself on Monday morning. Or maybe your mother should go with you."

There could only be one thing worse than depending on strangers, Kitty thought, and that was showing up in her new school with her mother and father, as if she were a baby in kindergarten. She could imagine the other children pointing to her and whispering and saying, "Look at that new girl" — and maybe even laughing. No, it was better to stumble along the hall on her own, looking lost perhaps, but at least not looking as if she was attached to a parent.

"No, thanks," said Kitty. "I can go alone."

Monday morning came quickly, even though Kitty had tried to keep awake on Sunday night in order to delay it as long as possible. Her father drank his coffee and gave her a warm hug as he left for the office. "You're sure you want to go alone?" he asked.

Kitty did not want to go alone at all. And she did not want to go with a parent. She simply did not want to go, period. She wondered how long it would be before she would be discovered if she did *not* go to school, but hid in some park or department store instead. Or maybe went back to Saint James and told Sister John Bosco it was all a mistake; they were not moving, after all. The nun at Saint Anthony's would probably just cross her name off the list and say, "Maybe she went to the public school instead."

Kitty brightened at the thought. She might never be missed. She could come home at three o'clock and make up a day in the classroom for her parents. She was good at that; she loved to make up stories. Her mother said she had an active imagination. She would have to be alert and inventive and make it all believable. It felt like a challenge!

"Drink your orange juice, Kitty," her mother was saying. "You don't want to come in late the first day. They may think you aren't coming at all."

Just exactly what she wanted. Not to be missed. She considered this daring move while her mother combed her hair again and straightened her skirt. Kitty's uniform had been ordered but would take six weeks to arrive. Meanwhile she had to wear regular clothes. Kitty had never worn regular clothes to school. It would be a good time *not* to go to school. She was unidentifiable without a Saint Anthony's or Saint James uniform on.

She took her new tablet her father had bought her and her newly sharpened pencil and started down Jefferson Avenue to Albert Street.

Kitty found her feet walking in the direction of school in spite of herself. Something deep inside told her she would eventually be found out and that some awful punishment would come to her if she was disobedient. She might even burn in the fires of hell some day long into the future, just for playing hooky. She could see herself, turned away from the gate of heaven — Saint Peter's lips grimly shut, his head shaking from side to side, his finger pointing the other direction. "What?" Kitty would say. "Just for that little sin when I was in third grade?" And Saint Peter would nod solemnly, his arms folded across her chest.

Kitty shivered. She kept walking toward Randolph Avenue. Happy children with friends passed her by, skipping and teasing and talking and laughing, just as Kitty had done at Saint James. She'd never felt so friendless as she did now. She was all alone on the face of the earth. She would never again have a friend. These were all total strangers. Alone, alone, alone. Third, fourth, fifth grade. Alone, alone, alone.

The patrol boy put up the sign for them to cross Randolph, and he sent one little boy back to the curb for running. The little boy looked as though he had tears in his eyes. Kitty wanted to put her arms around him and cry too.

On the playground the children stood around

in small groups, bright dots of blue sweaters and shiny waxed shoes, belonging. Kitty leaned against the fence and pretended to be reading her tablet. Pretended not to notice she was neglected. A ball rolled up to her feet. A boy's voice called, "Toss it over here, will you?" Kitty did. Two girls walked by arm in arm and smiled at her. On the teeter-totters, a boy was bouncing a girl up and down, high in the air. "Let me *down*," she screamed. The boy didn't. Suddenly the bell rang, and he got up and left, and the girl crashed to the ground in surprise.

Kitty followed the other children to the line that formed at the door. A nun who seemed to have no arms (they were slid into her full black sleeves) stood at the head of the line, staring. She appeared to be made of wood, she stood so still. As she stared, one by one the children stopped their hopping and bustling and whispering; and when the line was absolutely still, she lowered her chin to her chest. This seemed to be the signal for the line to enter the building. As the line got to the top of the stairs, each child headed for his classroom with a sense of purpose. As each one passed two wide doors in the middle of the hall, he made the sign of the cross and genuflected, and Kitty remembered that this was a school with a church plunk in the middle of it. Every time a person walked down the hall it looked as if he were tripping right in the middle.

Surely grade three would not be hard to find. But every door Kitty opened seemed to be another entrance to the church. Where in the world did they keep the school? Finally Kitty opened a door that showed a room with children in it. The desks were very small, and so were the students. GRADE ONE was printed on the door in small letters that Kitty had not seen.

"Pardon me," said Kitty, as she backed out into the hall. The door next door was second grade, the next must be the third. But it wasn't. It was the library. Kitty began to panic. She had obediently come on time (against her will), and now she was going to be late anyway.

She ran now, down the hall. The church again! The first grade room again! She was back

24

where she'd started. A patrol boy was just coming in from the street, and she called in desperation, "Where is the third grade?"

He pointed to the steps at the end of the hall. "Upstairs," he said, and Kitty sped up the steps quickly, forgetting even to thank him.

GRADE THREE said a sign on the door at the top of the steps. A line was going in and Kitty joined it. Everyone in the line went directly to a desk. Kitty stood by the door, waiting for Sister to say, "Welcome, Katherine. This is your seat here by the window," and after only slight stares Kitty would take her seat quickly and quietly and fade in with the rest of the class. But Sister did not say those words. She didn't say anything to her. The children stood for prayer (a prayer that Kitty had never heard of) and then saluted the flag. After that was an additional prayer for peace to Our Lady of Fatima, who warned of terrible war if people did not say the rosary.

Kitty did not know whether to join in with the flag salute (which she knew) or remain silent. No one seemed to notice if she did or didn't. A few people in the back of the room turned and looked at her, as if they might notice a piece of furniture out of place.

"Now!" said this strange nun (and about time, Kitty thought). "Let us take out our geography books."

Everyone else had a geography book and took it out. Now a few people in the front of the room turned around and looked at Kitty. And Kitty stood waiting.

"Oh my, I forgot attendance," said this flighty nun. She took out a gray attendance book and looked up and down the aisles.

Now she will notice me, thought Kitty. She could hardly avoid it. And there would be a note in her book, surely, that said she had a new pupil today. Unless the principal was as remiss as this nun.

"Karen?" said Sister, looking around the room, her gaze grazing Kitty's head. "Does anyone know where Karen is? Late? Sick?" Heads shook. Eyes checked the room. "And Edward, where is

Edward today?" At Saint James when pupils were missing from school, it was assumed they were ill, and no questions were asked. Sister John Bosco (what a *fine teacher*) simply put a check by their names, and when they had recovered they returned without fanfare.

A hand was waving. "Yes, Charles."

"I think Edward's got measles," said Charles, proud to offer some insight into the absentee problem.

Sister's eyebrows rose. "Indeed?" she said. "That will mean we all shall have measles soon, I suppose." She frowned at the thought of the gaps in her lesson plans. Could she go on with Africa and little Bambo, or should she wait?

Kitty wondered if Sister was planning on getting the measles, too. She had said "we" instead of "you." Surely nuns did not get measles.

"All right then," said Sister brightly. "We will turn to page fourteen." She had decided to press on with Bambo.

Kitty could not believe she was invisible.

What kind of a teacher could not see someone standing in her room? She wondered if she should raise her hand. Instead of that, she sneezed. Everyone turned around now.

Sister's eyebrows went up. They seemed to indicate a question. Nuns could do a lot with their eyebrows. Sometimes they had to say hardly any words.

"Yes?" said this Sister now. "Do you have a message from the office, dear?" She looked at Kitty at last.

Kitty shook her head.

"Is it about milk money?" said Sister. "I'm sorry, I forgot to collect it. Will the people with milk money come to my desk please."

Children untied corners of handkerchiefs and reached into pockets and lunch boxes. They formed another line at the desk, while Kitty shook her head again. *"No!"* she said. "It's not milk money."

Her voice rang out as clear as the soloist in the quiet church on Sunday morning at Saint James. Now she definitely had Sister's attention.

"Well then, speak up, what is it you want?" said Sister, a little crossly, Kitty thought.

"I'm new," said Kitty. When she said it she realized it sounded as if she was a newly minted penny, or a Sunday dress just purchased at the Golden Rule.

"New?" said this nun. "New?"

"I'm from Saint James, and I'm supposed to start school here today." Kitty was getting braver, because she was more and more annoyed now at the way Saint Anthony's seemed to be run.

Sister left the milk line where it was standing and took out her attendance book. She asked Kitty her name. She frowned as she looked down the rows of names, and then she said, "I'm sorry, I don't have your name here. I was not notified of anyone new in this room."

A few children snickered. A few others looked puzzled along with Sister, and their eyes followed the conversation between the two.

"Are you sure you are in third grade?" Sister said.

Now Kitty *was* dismayed. As if she didn't

know how old she was, or what grade she was in. Next she would be asked if she knew her own name.

"I am sure," she said.

"Perhaps you should go to the office and check with Sister Justina. Just go downstairs and turn left and you will see the office."

Kitty felt relieved to get out of the room and worried that she would be sent back once the records were straight. After all, she did have to attend third grade. Where else could she go?

The halls were silent now. Not another person was in sight. Behind the closed doors were children who had their own desks and books and crayons and friends and private jokes. They belonged here. Kitty did not belong here. She was a trespasser just wandering through a cold concrete hallway, which seemed bigger by far than Saint James. Even bigger than it had seemed this morning when there were other children in it. She could just keep on walking right out the door and no one would chase after her, no one would say, "Come back!" She would not ever, ever be missed. She did not remember when she had ever felt so alone as she did now in this big, cold hallway. Her steps echoed in her ears.

Kitty saw the office and decided to walk right by and out the door. If they didn't want her, it was fine with her. She had given them a chance, she had come to school, and no one wanted her. She did not have to go to school. She knew how to read. School was a waste of time anyway.

But just as she was pulling the big heavy door open (even the doors resisted her in this school) she heard a voice echo behind her. "Where are you going, dear?" it said.

Saint Anthony's must be on the watch for escaping pupils, thought Kitty, without looking to see who was behind her. Perhaps others have tried to get away, too. Kitty thought it must be like this in jail. So close to freedom, and then at the last minute someone captures you.

"Your name wouldn't be Katherine, would it?" said the voice, now closer. The owner of the voice appeared at her side, and put a large, black-draped arm around her shoulder. It smelled like Sister John Bosco, but then, Kitty decided, all nuns must smell alike.

"Yes!" said Kitty. "My name is Katherine!" Kitty felt warm toward this nun who knew her name.

"We've been looking all morning for you," Sister said. "I am Sister Justina, and we expected you to come to the office this morning."

"I went to the third grade," said Kitty. "I am in third grade, you know. But I wasn't on the list in third grade."

"That is because you are in the *other* third grade," said Sister Justina. "We have two third grades this year because there were too many children for one."

A church inside of a school, and two third grades. Kitty wondered what other surprises life at Saint Anthony's would bring.

3

"Second" Communion Practice

The principal led Kitty back up the stairs, with a black sleeve enveloping and directing her. The sleeve was so big and loose that it almost covered Kitty from head to toe. Kitty felt like a small nun walking with a big one. Sister's other hand fingered the beads around her waist. They passed right by the "wrong" third grade and went to the other end of the hall. At Saint James, only the upperclassmen had rooms upstairs. Sixth, seventh, and eighth grades. Here Kitty was already upstairs, in only the third grade! She felt very grown up.

Sister tapped on a classroom door. It was immediately opened by a girl with long sausage curls who, Kitty noticed, looked spotlessly neat and clean. When she saw Sister Justina the girl clapped her hands lightly and the whole class stood up beside their desks and said, "Good morning, Sister Justina."

Sister Justina made motions with her hands (palms down) and the whole class sat down. "Good morning, boys and girls. This is Katherine, a new third grader, whom I hope you will make very welcome here at Saint Anthony's."

Kitty felt her face turn very red. She crept out from under Sister Justina's sleeve and shook another hand attached to another black sleeve, as the principal said, "Sister Charlene will be your teacher, Katherine."

"It's good to have new blood in the class," said Sister Charlene. "Margaret Mary, could you make room for Katherine to sit with you for the morning? You can show her where we are in our workbooks, and tomorrow we'll give her a desk of her own."

Margaret Mary was the neat, sausage-curled girl who had answered the door. She moved quickly over in her desk and made room for Kitty. Then she took out her workbooks and showed her what to do and made room for her tablet and pencil inside the desk. Margaret Mary had a small dust rag folded inside her desk that she took out frequently to brush away any dust or eraser-shavings or chalk dust that had accumulated on the surface. Kitty could see that she was a serious student. Her workbooks were done in small, even handwriting, with no crossed-out words or smeared pencil marks. At the top of every completed page was a gold star, placed there (Kitty was sure) by Sister Charlene. Margaret Mary wore a brown scapular under her blouse (Kitty could just see the edge of the brown cord at the neck) and a Miraculous Medal on a silver chain over it.

Sister Justina went to the door, and the whole class again stood up and said, "Good-bye, Sister Justina." The principal waved, moving three of her fingers at them, as she left the room.

Kitty followed along with Margaret Mary during each lesson. When Sister asked how much nine times eight was, she knew but didn't feel brave enough yet to raise her hand. It would be too easy to do or say some "Saint James" thing that would make Saint Anthony pupils laugh. She would wait until she knew the rules.

Sister called on a boy named Virgil.

"Fourteen," he answered. The class twittered.

Sister sighed. She called on Margaret Mary. (Kitty noticed she always called on Margaret Mary when no one else knew the answer. She never called on her first. It seemed Margaret Mary could always be depended on to know.)

"Seventy-two, Sister," said Margaret Mary, standing up to answer and sitting down when she'd finished.

"I just wish I had more Margaret Marys in the class," said Sister Charlene.

There had been a "Margaret Mary" in Kitty's room at Saint James too. Her name was Roberta, and she never had been known to give a wrong answer or get anything less than an A on her report card.

The day wore on, and Kitty noticed that whenever she looked up, the boys and girls were looking at her. She felt very much out of place sitting at someone else's desk, among strange children and unfamiliar surroundings and textbooks. And most of all, she felt conspicuous as the only one in the room out of uniform. Everyone in the whole room was in navy blue except Kitty, who stood out brightly in her plaid skirt and red sweater. Even if no one wanted to look at her, they couldn't help it. A person's eye was drawn to red, when it was the only red thing in the room.

"Now!" Sister Charlene was saying. "We will line up in the correct order to go to church for first communion practice." The class sighed. They found first communion practice every day very boring.

Kitty wasn't bored. She was in a panic. She had already made her first communion. She raised her hand to tell Sister this, but by now there was a scramble to find the right places in line. The shortest people were headed for the front of the line, the tallest for the back.

Kitty knew better than to disobey nuns. If Sister said to get in line, she had to get in line. Slipping into line in a place where everyone seemed to be her height, she wondered if it was possible to make her first communion twice. Or would this be called her "second" communion? She felt as if it could be a sin.

Kitty continued to wave her hand, anxious to let Sister know that she did not belong here. But Sister was going over rules now for fasting for communion. Kitty knew all the rules. Then she told the girls about how to buy dresses and veils and mother-of-pearl–covered prayer books and rosaries. Kitty knew all this too. She had a dress and veil at home hanging in the closet from Saint James. At Saint James, children made their first communion in second grade. Saint Anthony's seemed to be behind in some things.

When everyone's hands were folded and heads were bowed the procession started down the stairs toward the church. They filed into the front pews, six to a pew, while they sang some Latin song that Kitty did not know. Kitty felt like a very bright flower in the middle of a meadow, the only one not singing, and the only one in red.

Two by two the children came to the front of the church, while Sister pretended she was Father Bauer and placed an imaginary host on each child's outstretched tongue. Kitty wanted to raise her hand when her turn came, but Sister had told them to keep hands folded. She couldn't just blurt words out without raising her hand; in fact, she couldn't say words at all. It was a sin to talk in church. So Kitty whispered. While her tongue was out in the proper position, she said: "I can't make my first communion!"

Sister looked startled. But just for a moment. Then she said, softly, "You don't have a dress and veil?"

Kitty shook her head vehemently.

"Don't worry," said Sister Charlene to Kitty. "The Lord works in strange ways."

For the second time this month Kitty had been told this! She wondered if it was something the nuns learned in the convent. If two nuns said it, it must be true. But from what Kitty had seen of the Lord's strange ways, it was not very encouraging. Now Sister Charlene thought she had no dress and veil for communion. When Kitty shook her head "no," she meant Sister's statement was wrong: She *did* have a dress and veil. Sister Charlene took it to mean No, I *don't* have a dress and veil! Kitty tried to explain this to her, but Sister was motioning her along because the next first communicant was edging up to her with his mouth open and tongue out. The look in Sister's eye said that church was no place for a conversation, especially on the altar step.

Finally the rehearsal was over for the day, and the class filed back to the classroom. Sister taught a spelling lesson (easier words than they had at Saint James) and an arithmetic lesson (harder problems than at Saint James), and then Margaret Mary handed Kitty a library book to read about Saint Joan of Arc. Kitty tried to concentrate on the story, but her mind kept worrying back to the first communion problem and how to solve it.

Just then there was a tap on the door, and a messenger girl from one of the older grades came in carrying a first communion dress and veil. She handed it to Sister Charlene, and some whispered conversation took place. When she'd gone, Sister turned around and said "Kitty?"

Kitty looked up in surprise.

"Here is something for you, dear. All your worries are over." She handed Kitty the dress and veil. Her face looked bright and pleased. She had a you-don't-have-to-thank-me look.

Kitty made no move to take the dress. Even if she'd needed a dress she would not have taken it. It looked gray and dingy and worn, and the veil was old-fashioned and limp. How could Sister Charlene think she would wear that, anyway?

Sister shook the dress and veil at her. Kitty felt ungrateful and embarrassed.

"Here!" said Sister. "You can have it, it is yours! Don't worry about paying. It is yours!"

Suddenly it was more than Kitty could stand. She stood up and heard herself shout, "I don't want it! I don't need a dress! I made my first communion last year in second grade at Saint James!" She felt her face grow red and flushed. But she'd said it, she'd told Sister the truth, and there could be no misunderstanding about the facts now.

Sister drew the dress and veil back. She looked shocked and a little hurt. Kitty felt she had perhaps been too hard on Sister.

"Thank you," said Kitty, "but I don't need it. I made my communion." It did not hurt to repeat the statement, just to be sure Sister heard. The class was agog, and clearly enjoying the diversion. It was not every day that something this exciting happened, having Sister Charlene's generosity rejected.

"Well," said Sister. "Why didn't you *tell* me this before?"

"I tried," said Kitty.

Sister handed the dress to Margaret Mary and said, "Take this to the office." The dress looked limper than ever on its hanger and seemed to have lost all of its promise.

"Yes, Sister," said Margaret Mary, obediently.

"When we have communion practice in the future," said Sister Charlene, who did not like her offers to be rejected, "you will sit here in the classroom and read a library book."

"Yes, Sister," said Kitty.

Although everyone was still looking at Kitty, and she still did not know anyone in the room, Kitty felt better than she had all day. It was as if there had been some kind of quiet battle, and she had won. The first day of school was over, and Kitty had won.

4
New Friends

The next morning when Kitty got to school, Margaret Mary was waiting for her on the playground.

"Don't you go to mass in the morning?" she said, running up to Kitty.

"Do we have to?" said Kitty in alarm, thinking that she had missed out on some of the rules.

"No, we don't *have* to, but my mother says we should do good things out of love, not because we have to. It's a good chance to gain indulgences for the poor souls in purgatory."

Kitty had never known anyone who cared about the poor souls in purgatory. The priests and nuns always talked about them, and everyone knew you *should* care about them, but Kitty had never met anyone who really did. Margaret Mary seemed to really care.

"Maybe I'll go," said Kitty.

If Margaret Mary went to daily mass she probably liked to have friends who did, too. It would be a small price for Kitty to pay to have a friend.

"Do lots of people go every morning?" said Kitty.

Margaret Mary shook her head. "No," she admitted. "Only about ten people in the whole church. And Our Lady warned us that the world would have to turn to prayer, or it would be taken over by communism."

It seemed that Margaret Mary took everything to heart, thought Kitty. Kitty did not know anything about communism, but if it was as bad as that, she probably should go to mass. On the other hand, if only ten people went to mass every morning, it couldn't be a very *popular* thing to do. Nine of the people were probably nuns, and the tenth was Margaret Mary, the only one not wearing black. Kitty might not make many other friends if she was too holy. Maybe she would go one day a week. That would be holy but not *too* holy. If it didn't help all of the poor souls in purgatory, it may help one a week, with a little left over for communism.

Kitty and Margaret Mary sat on the swings and exchanged facts about their families. Margaret Mary came from a large family. She had lots of responsibilities around the house and helped her mother sew, preserve food, cook, and clean.

"My mother says I'll thank her someday when I have a house and children of my own."

Kitty had not thought about her "own" home, or her own children. She had trouble just washing her hair alone and making the part straight. She'd never be able to cook her own meals (Kitty's mother said she left a mess in the kitchen when she made a snack) or iron her clothes. Margaret Mary was definitely going to be a friend who would be hard to live up to.

"See that girl?" said Margaret Mary. She nodded her head toward the fence, because it was not polite to point.

Kitty looked in the direction she nodded. There was a girl Kitty recognized from their room, with light brown hair that looked red in the sun. She was standing with three boys, laughing and talking.

"She's boy crazy," said Margaret Mary. "I don't like to gossip, but you wouldn't want to go around with her. My mother says people are judged by the company they keep."

Kitty watched the girl. She appeared to be having a good time. Kitty wondered if Margaret Mary ever had a good time.

"Her name is Ruthie," Margaret Mary added.

Just then the bell rang, and everyone ran to get into line. When they got to their room, Sister Charlene had a desk ready for Kitty, with fresh clean workbooks and other supplies. It was on the other side of the room from Margaret Mary, near the window and halfway down the row.

Kitty put her tablet and pencil into her desk next to the new workbooks and looked around her. Across from her sat a girl with a plain face and a rather dirty uniform. It looked as if she had spilled some of her lunch on it, or maybe several lunches. Her hair looked stringy. There had been a girl at Saint James who had looked like this, and no one played with her at recess.

Ahead of Kitty were two boys who seemed to be very studious. They were probably competitors of Margaret Mary's.

Kitty felt a tap on the shoulder. She turned around, and a girl with bouncy blond curls tied with a pink ribbon said, "Do you want to come over to my house and play Confession?"

Kitty had never heard of playing Confession. Confession was a sacrament for forgiving sins — Kitty had made her first confession last year. To play Confession sounded a bit sacrilegious, but fun. She had a feeling Margaret Mary would not play Confession. She also had a feeling that this girl was not a friend of Margaret Mary's.

"Yes," whispered Kitty.

"When?" whispered the girl. "How about the day after tomorrow, after school?"

"Fine," said Kitty.

The girl wrote her name and address on a piece of paper. She reached over Kitty's shoulder and dropped it onto her desk. The girl's name was Eileen. Kitty liked her. Just the thought of playing Confession made her spine tingle. Eileen seemed to be someone it would be fun to have for a friend. Dangerous maybe, but fun.

"Eileen!" said Sister Charlene in a loud voice. "We wouldn't want to set a bad example for our new girl, would we?"

"No, Sister," said Eileen, in a flat, uninterested voice.

"Let us not pass any more notes in class," Sister added.

"Yes, Sister," said Eileen in the same flat tone.

"Come right from school," whispered Eileen, her voice close to the back of Kitty's neck. "Get in my line with me."

Kitty nodded. Eileen did not seem to worry about being a bad example, or about the promise she had just made to Sister Charlene. If she, Kitty, had been reprimanded, worry would plague her every minute!

Just then another note dropped onto Kitty's desk from over her shoulder. Eileen was very brazen! "Ask your mom if you can stay for dinner," the note read.

Dinner! Eileen must mean *supper*. Lunchtime was at noon. It would be after three o'clock when they'd go to Eileen's house. She was invited to supper at someone's house who called supper "dinner"! Just the way they did in the movies.

"My dad will drive you home," whispered Eileen again, into Kitty's hair.

By this time Kitty had lost her place in the geography book, and Margaret Mary was standing up answering Sister's question about the climate in Bambo's country. Kitty's mind was on Eileen's father's car. Kitty's father did not drive. Not many people Kitty knew had cars. Aunt Jo was the only one in the family who did — she had a 1939 Chevrolet.

But Eileen's family owned a car, and her father did not mind giving Eileen's friends rides home. Eileen had not even asked him yet: She must just take for granted that he would do this. Why, he didn't even know where Kitty lived!

"Eileen?" said Sister Charlene. "What is the principal export of Bambo's country?"

"I have no idea, Sister," said Eileen, as uninterested as ever.

The class twittered.

Sister rattled her wooden rosary beads around her waist in an obvious attempt to control her impatience. "Perhaps," she said pointedly, "you should look in your geography book so you will get an idea."

"Yes, Sister," said Eileen, her curls bouncing.

Sister looked around the room at the waving

hands — hands belonging to people who knew all about Bambo and his country.

"Kitty?" said Sister lightly. "Can you please tell us the answer?"

Kitty felt her face turn bright red. Before she could think, she blurted out, "My hand wasn't up, Sister." What kind of nun would call on someone who was not volunteering the answer? Besides that, a new girl on her second day in school could not be expected to know answers already. Why, at Saint James they had never heard of Bambo.

Sister looked surprised. "I am aware that your hand was not raised, Katherine. I do not just call on people who have their hands up. It is everyone's duty to pay attention and know the answer."

It was a trick then. Sister *deliberately* called on people who did not know the answer. To embarrass them perhaps, and teach them a lesson! Kitty longed for Saint James and dear Sister John Bosco, who never tricked innocent children. A person could never feel safe in class now, thought

Kitty. At any moment, hand up or not, Sister Charlene could make your name ring out and hang in the air while everyone turned to stare. It felt unfair to Kitty, something that happened in public schools perhaps, but not here where nuns (her father said) gave up their lives to bring truth to small children. Kitty thought sadly that perhaps there was no one who could be trusted. No one in the entire world.

The thought was so overwhelming to Kitty that she felt like crying, but she did not want to be the center of attention again so she squeezed her eyes together tightly to block the tears. Kitty's feelings always got in the way. On the other hand, Eileen, who certainly had something to cry about, having been chastised by Sister, was humming a movie tune under her breath and drawing pictures in the margin of her catechism. Margaret Mary was standing up again answering another of Sister's unanswered questions. And no one else in the room seemed to worry about being called on, or the fact that no one in the world could be trusted.

Finally the bell rang and the day was over. Kitty waved to Eileen, who lived in the opposite direction, and set off toward Jefferson Avenue, in the line with Margaret Mary.

"Do you like paper dolls?" said Margaret Mary, as they walked along Albert Street.

Kitty nodded. "I love them," she said. "I've got *Gone With the Wind* and Deanna Durbin and Lana Turner."

Margaret Mary frowned. "I only like baby paper dolls," she said. "My mother says the movie star paper dolls are too mature for children our age."

"I like baby dolls too!" said Kitty. "I've got Baby Snooks and a Dydee doll book!"

"Would you like to come over after school tomorrow and play with them?" asked Margaret Mary. "My mother lets me bring home a guest sometimes, if I ask her ahead of time."

"I'll ask my mother," said Kitty, excited at the prospect of going to two new Saint Anthony friends' homes in such a short time.

Kitty turned up Jefferson Avenue, and waved

to Margaret Mary, who continued on to Saint Clair.

That night when she told her father about Sister Charlene's trickery, he patted her on the head and said, "You take life too seriously, Kitty. Much, much too seriously. Life is not really serious at all, you know. You must try hard never to hurt anyone, and after that you should just have a good time." Kitty wanted to believe her father's words, but she didn't know how to have a good time. She felt like crying about this, too! And how could her father, who was very serious himself, tell her life was all fun?

When Kitty turned off the lamp beside her bed, she made up her mind to think only of things that were fun. She remembered that she had made two new friends already, and that her mother had given her permission to go to Margaret Mary's house right from school, and the next day to go to Eileen's and stay for dinner (if Eileen's mother invited her). Those two things should balance out any of the grim ones that would surely come up soon.

5

An After-School Visit

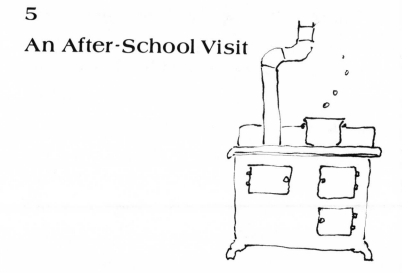

The next day at school passed quickly by, without Sister Charlene tricking Kitty by calling on her when her hand was not raised. Kitty had her paper dolls in a Fanny Farmer box in her school bag ready to go to Margaret Mary's after school. At three o'clock the girls got in line together and walked right past Jefferson Avenue and on to Saint Clair.

Margaret Mary's house was large and old, with a broad front porch across the front. Even before they went in the back door, Kitty could smell food cooking. She could not identify the smell. It was nothing familiar, but when they entered the kitchen Kitty saw that it came from something simmering in a large kettle on the back of a black wood stove. Margaret Mary's mother, who was wearing a flowered apron and had gray hair, was stirring it. The stove made the kitchen very warm, and Margaret Mary's mother's face was red. She wiped it every few minutes with a hanky from her apron pocket.

Margaret Mary gave her mother a kiss and said, "Mother, this is Kitty, the new girl at school."

"God bless you, my dear," said Margaret Mary's mother, reaching out a rough red hand to shake Kitty's small pink one.

So this is the mother who knows so much, thought Kitty. Whom Margaret Mary is always quoting. She did not look the way Kitty expected. Kitty realized that she had imagined her as a sort of combination of the nuns she knew — perhaps with a short black veil.

Margaret Mary also introduced Kitty to her father, who was just leaving for work (in the middle of the afternoon?) with a black metal lunch box. His hair was slicked back and his clothes didn't look as if they had been purchased at The Golden Rule, where Kitty's father's suits were from.

Kitty met Margaret Mary's brother Eddy and her sisters and her Aunt Edith and Uncle Hiram. There seemed to be no end of relatives milling about. It felt as if it was a holiday. Holidays were the only time there were this many people at Kitty's house.

"Is it someone's birthday?" whispered Kitty to her new friend.

"No," said Margaret Mary.

"Then why are they all here?" asked Kitty.

Margaret Mary looked puzzled. "They live here," she said.

Live here! All of these people lived in one house? Kitty sat on a kitchen chair and watched Margaret Mary peeling carrots. The other people were all peeling something or stirring something, and sounds of someone playing the piano came from the front hall. On every wall there was a religious picture. Behind Kitty was the Sacred Heart, with braided blessed palm in back of it, and across from her was a painting of the Last Supper. In a place Margaret Mary called the pantry hung a small holy water font, like those in church, only smaller, and everyone who passed in and out of the room dipped their fingers in the holy water and made the sign of the cross. Kitty had never seen a holy water fountain except in church.

"There!" said Margaret Mary, putting the carrot peelings in a garbage can. "Now we can play."

"Better get at your homework," said Margaret Mary's mother.

"We will," said Margaret Mary.

Kitty followed Margaret Mary up a wide staircase in the front hall to her bedroom. The bedroom had a holy water font too, and four beds in a row. "This is mine," she said, pointing to the one on the end. "Those are my sisters' beds."

From under the bed she took out a box with paper dolls in it. "Maybe we should do our homework first," she said.

Kitty always did her homework after supper, with her father. She could not imagine doing it with a friend. Margaret Mary must do hers alone, thought Kitty. Kitty's mind was spinning. The smell of the food cooking downstairs was very strong in the bedroom.

"Hungarian goulash," said Margaret Mary, noticing that Kitty was sniffing the air.

"You're welcome to stay for supper," she added. "My mom says there is always room for one more at our table."

"I'd have to call my mother and ask," said Kitty. "Or she'd worry."

"We don't have a telephone," said Margaret Mary.

Somehow Kitty was not surprised Margaret Mary did not have a telephone. Her house felt so old-fashioned with its black stove and holy pictures and row of beds in the bedroom and holy water fonts that a phone would be too modern. Kitty would have to turn down the invitation to eat Hungarian goulash. She felt sad about it. She was beginning to like the big noisy family and the good smells and warm relatives. Kitty's house felt empty by comparison. Margaret Mary must never have a chance to be lonely with so many people about every day.

Kitty mused on how it would feel to share a room with three people, and share the cooking and housework. She could not even imagine how she would feel if she lived here. At home she was an only child and never had to share anything. She was always the most important one and had all of her parents' attention. Still, there seemed to be enough love in this house to go around. Margaret Mary did not seem to be unloved.

Kitty and Margaret Mary did a little homework together, and then they played with their paper dolls.

"I like paper dolls," said Margaret Mary, "but I don't get a chance to play with them often, because there is so much work to do. And I have to study because my mother likes me to keep my grades high."

Margaret Mary's grades were high. Kitty knew that. She was the smartest one in the third grade. Kitty didn't care whether her grades were high or not. It seemed an awful lot of work to get A's. She thought that Eileen might feel the same way.

After paper dolls, Margaret Mary played the piano for Kitty (she took lessons at the convent), and then all of the family began setting the dining room table and getting things ready for supper.

"You are welcome to stay and eat with us," said Margaret Mary's mother. "There's always enough for one more."

Kitty thanked her, saying that her own mother was expecting her, and got ready to leave. Margaret Mary walked her out to the alley and said, "I'll see you tomorrow morning on the corner for mass."

Kitty agreed and, waving good-bye, started

down Albert Street toward Jefferson. As she walked she looked back at Margaret Mary's house. The lights were just coming on, and it looked warm and cozy. The smell of the goulash lingered in Kitty's memory. And she felt pleased that she had a surprise for her father — part of her homework was already done!

6

Dinner at Suppertime

At mass the next morning, Kitty decided that she had to be a saint. She had gotten up early for mass and met Margaret Mary at the corner. Margaret Mary was carrying her daily missal with silk ribbons marking the parts of the mass, along with her blue crystal rosary in a case. It was so early that the sun was only half up, and the streets looked deserted. People were probably sleeping inside all of the houses she passed, Kitty thought. She felt especially virtuous, pioneer-like, going to daily mass.

Kitty had her first communion prayer book with her, with its mother-of-pearl cover and real cross pasted to a little shrine on the first page. She showed it to Margaret Mary.

"It's nice," said Margaret Mary. "But a little childish."

Kitty felt defensive. After all, they *were* children. Children could be childish. In fact, they *should* be childish. Besides, missals were for adults. It was like wearing your mother's shoes.

"This is the only way to follow daily mass," said Margaret Mary. She tapped her missal. "All the Latin is right here; you can follow right along with the priest. And all the feast days. When Father reads the gospel, you read it with him."

Kitty could not see any particular merit in reading along with the priest. It was fine just to listen. Kitty had enough trouble reading the English words in a prayer book. She did not feel like trying to read Latin.

Margaret Mary went on. "My mother says it is best to learn right from the start. It's like learning to type. You should start with a real typewriter, not one of those toy ones. Or a piano. Some kids have those little things, but I started learning right away on our big one."

Kitty was not sure she could see the connection between pianos and typewriters and missals, but she knew Margaret Mary's mother must know.

When mass began, Kitty did feel childish with her small prayer book with the large print, while Margaret Mary and all the nuns around them flipped the ribbon-marked pages in accord with the priest and appeared to be very professional church-goers. They even mouthed the Latin responses with the altar boys.

At the sermon, Father Bauer spoke about everyone's calling to be a saint. "Sainthood," he said, looking right at Kitty, "Is not just for noble people who lived years ago. Every single person who goes to heaven is a saint!" Here Father Bauer slammed down his own missal on the lectern for emphasis. "On the other hand," he went on, "if you die in mortal sin, then you go directly to hell." (Here Father Bauer pointed down at the floor.)

Kitty shuddered. This was serious business. How could her father possibly think life was all fun?

"Forever," Father Bauer added. "Infinity is longer than we can even imagine."

Just when Kitty was ready to burst into tears, Father Bauer extended his arms, draping the sleeves of his vestments like a large curtain, and said, "The choice is up to you! You can obey the commandments and be a saint forever in heaven with God" — he paused — "or burn forever in the fire of hell."

As Father Bauer went on with the mass, Kitty knew there was no choice. She surely would not burn forever in hell. She *had* to be a saint. She simply had to go to heaven!

After mass, Kitty told Margaret Mary that she had to be a saint.

"Of course," said Margaret Mary. "That is why we were born."

Margaret Mary made it all sound so simple.

"But don't you ever worry that you will commit a bad sin and die before you can go to confession?"

Margaret Mary shook her head. "I don't commit sins."

Kitty looked at her with respect. She believed her. Kitty wished that she could feel as confident as that about sin, but bad things seemed to be lurking around every corner to trap her. Somehow she knew that even though she kept trying to be a saint, she would unknowingly disobey Sister or her mother, or tell a lie on the spur of the moment, and then be struck down by a car on the way home from school.

She looked at the cars driving by the schoolyard. They seemed to be a menace. And even lightning could hit her — there were many bad storms in Minnesota. It seemed hopeless. She would have to remember every single waking moment that she had to be a saint. Life seemed so much harder at Saint Anthony's than it had at Saint James. Or maybe it was just that she was getting older and it was harder to be an adult than a child.

Kitty tried all day long to be a saint. She had a lot of time to think about it, because the class went to church again for first communion practice, and Kitty was left sitting in the classroom with her library book about Saint Joan of Arc. In front of her on the wall was a picture of hell. The fire was bright and red, redder than the fire her dad made when he burned the autumn leaves on the curb in front of their house. Sister said it was there to remind the children of the punishment for sin.

Kitty was so deep in thought, she hardly heard the class return from church.

"Get in line with me when the bell rings," whispered Eileen, at three o'clock. Kitty nodded. She couldn't tell Eileen she'd changed her mind now. Besides, she wanted friends and she wanted very badly to go to someone's house who played Confession and ate dinner in the evening.

"Whoopee!" shouted Eileen, as soon as they

were a short way from school. She threw her books high into the air, and they landed in a muddy ditch when they came down. "I hate being cramped up in school all day, don't you?" she said.

Kitty nodded. "I hate it," she said. She heard her own words and wondered why she said it. She didn't hate school. She didn't *love* it, but she didn't hate it either. Especially now that she had friends.

And now she had told a lie. A lie was a *sin!*

"This looks like one block." Eileen was chattering away in the background, referring to the open grassy field they were crossing behind the school on the way to her house. "But it is really about four blocks. The streets don't go through on Albert, but it is still four blocks."

Back over her shoulder Kitty could see Saint Anthony's — and up ahead, Eileen pointed out her house. There was nothing but open fields in between. Kitty was wondering what the difference was — why it mattered to Eileen if it was one block, or four.

"Kids who live close to school," Eileen went on, "have to go home for lunch. But if you live more than four blocks away, you can stay. I think I should be able to take my lunch. But Sister said last year that I only live one block from school. It's not fair."

"That's mean," agreed Kitty, feeling sympathy for Eileen even though she wondered why she'd want to bring her lunch to school.

"It's really cold in the winter," Eileen continued. "And if I go home at noon, that is sixteen blocks altogether I have to walk in the snow and the wind."

Eileen didn't look delicate. She was racing ahead now, turning cartwheels in the long grass.

When they got to Eileen's house, her mother was waiting at the door. She welcomed Kitty warmly and gave Eileen a big hug and asked her how her school day was. She seemed so *glad* to see her. Kitty wished that her mother would hug her like that when she got home. But instead she usually said, "Did you wipe your feet?" and sent Kitty back to make sure there was no dirt

71

on her shoes. Eileen's mother did not seem to care about dirt. Yet when they got inside, the house was spotless.

"We have a cleaning lady that comes in every week," said Eileen when Kitty asked.

A cleaning lady! No one Kitty knew had a cleaning lady! People in New York or Hollywood had cleaning ladies, not people in Saint Paul!

Instead of leaving the room as Kitty's mother did when she had friends over, Eileen's mother sat down with them in the living room and listened to Eileen's tales of the day. When Eileen told her how mean Sister Charlene was and how she hadn't even let Eileen pass Kitty a note with her name on it her mother made sympathetic noises with her tongue, as if she *agreed!* Kitty's mother and father would have told her the nuns were holy women who gave up their lives to teach impatient children, and Margaret Mary's mother (Kitty supposed) would have said they were lucky to be getting such a fine education. But Eileen's mother sympathized with Eileen!

And she seemed to actually like being with the girls. She asked Kitty how she was enjoying her new home and school, and if she had any brothers and sisters (What? An only child? Just like Eileen!), and how far from school she lived. (This seemed to be an important point to Eileen's family.)

Then she put another log on the fire (a real fire in a real fireplace!) and went to the kitchen and brought small glasses of grape juice in on a silver tray, along with apples and a small plate of sandwiches with the crusts cut off. Kitty's mother made her eat the crust on her bread. Eileen's mother passed the tray to Kitty first as if she was very important, and it appeared that they were to eat right there in the living room in front of the fire, with no mention of crumbs that could fall on the oriental carpet or down the sides of the brocade sofa. From habit Kitty wanted to shout, "Grape juice stains!" but she caught herself just in time.

Alongside the fireplace were bookshelves — tall, dark bookshelves, filled with books of all kinds. Kitty's bookshelf at home held her story-book dolls on display. And in the corner a grandfather clock chimed a song every fifteen minutes, a mellow faraway song that sounded as if it was coming in from over the tops of snowcapped mountains. Kitty didn't want to move. She wanted to stay in this peaceful place forever. It felt so safe and far from nuns and priests and school and sin.

Eileen's mother seemed to be dressed up as if she was going out somewhere for the afternoon. But as the time passed, and she did not leave, Kitty wondered if she was dressed up for *her*, for *Kitty*. Or maybe this is what some mothers wore at home — a good dress and pearls around the neck and high-heeled shoes — just for every-day. To do the wash. Or perhaps they didn't do the wash. Along with the cleaning lady, they could have a washerwoman. Kitty's mind was spinning. How she envied Eileen! Eileen lived like a princess!

"We're going to play in my room," said Eileen, standing up suddenly. "Confession."

"Fine," said Eileen's mother, clearing the dishes away. "Have a good time!"

Have a good time! Kitty never told her mother what she was going to play. Especially if she was going to play something questionable like Confession. But Eileen's mother seemed to think it was the most ordinary thing in the world. Instead of saying, "Why don't you play dolls instead," she said, "Have a good time!" Kitty could see there was a lot to learn about other people's families.

"My mom is a convert," said Eileen, as they started for her room.

Before Kitty could absorb one shock, there was another. A convert for a mother. Kitty had never known a convert.

"She thought she may as well be Catholic. My dad was Catholic, and it's better for a family to be all one thing."

Eileen talked as if being Catholic was something you did for convenience, like joining a YWCA.

Eileen's room looked like the room of a

princess. It had white fluffy curtains on the windows and maple furniture that all matched. Her bed had a dotted-swiss spread with ruffles, and at the foot of the bed was a green satin comforter folded in a triangle, all puffy and fresh looking. Dolls in crisp dresses sat in rockers, waiting to be picked up and played with, and a bookcase with glass doors held *Black Beauty, Hans Brinker, Honey Bunch, Tom Sawyer, Huckleberry Finn,* and others. Kitty did not see a single "Lives of the Saints" book. In fact, not any religious book at all! Eileen's own little radio and clock stood humming away on a bedside table, and over her bed on a little shelf were some Hummel figures of children instead of a cross or a statue of the Blessed Virgin Mary.

Eileen began pushing furniture around. She took all of her clothes out of her closet and threw them on her bed. Then she shoved a chair and the bedside table into the closet. "A confessional has to be dark," she said. "We'll put this blanket up between the priest and the sinner."

Eileen seemed to take sin very lightly. Kitty

was sure she did not lie awake at night worrying about hell. And with all the noise of moving furniture, her mother did not once come in to see what the girls were doing.

"Now!" said Eileen. "Do you want to be the priest or the sinner?"

Kitty did not know how to answer a question like that. She never ever anticipated she'd be asked.

"I like to be the sinner," Eileen went on before Kitty answered. "Why don't you be the priest?"

Kitty sat on the chair in the dark corner of Eileen's closet and pulled the blanket in front of her. It smelled warm and rich, like the inside of her mother's cedar chest.

"Wait!" said Eileen. "I forgot. You need this robe on, you know, like that thing the priest wears." Eileen handed her a long lacy bathrobe.

"A surplice," said Kitty.

"Yeah. Whatever you call it," said Eileen. "Now, are you ready?"

Kitty didn't know what she had to do to be

ready. She said, "Yes," in a muffled voice.

"I'll just shut the door and get in line outside and when the other person is through, I'll come in. Make that kind of scraping noise like that little door sliding shut."

Eileen shut the closet door and went out. It was pitch dark. Kitty thought to herself how fast things changed. Only days ago she was a lonely new girl in school. Now here she was, a priest huddled in a new friend's black, black closet. The last place in the world she would have dreamed of. Life was fraught with surprise.

It was so peaceful in the warm, dark closet that Kitty got sleepy. She wanted to stay there forever. Before long she heard the door open. She heard Eileen kneel down at the bedside table which was no longer at the bedside.

"Slide the door open," she whispered.

Kitty slid the imaginary door open. She made the sign of the cross over Eileen's shadowy form.

"Bless me Father, for I have sinned," said Eileen confidently.

"My last confession was ten years ago, and these are my sins."

"Ten years?" shrieked Kitty. "How could it be ten years?"

"I'm a grownup," said Eileen. "I'm not a child. And I'm a bad sinner."

Kitty was certainly not used to playing grownup games.

"And you're a real old priest. Old and crabby. You're really going to be *mad* when you hear my sins.

"And these are my sins," repeated Eileen dramatically. Kitty waited expectantly.

"I ate meat on Friday thirty-six times," said Eileen. "And I didn't go to church on Sunday twenty-four times. I got divorced twice, and I had impure thoughts nineteen times."

"Wow," said Kitty from behind the blanket. "*No* one is that bad, Eileen."

"Yes, they are," said Eileen cheerfully. "My aunt *never* goes to mass. And lots of people eat meat on Friday."

Kitty didn't know any. Eileen must know actual pagans.

"But you're s'posed to be *mad*," said Eileen. "A priest would be really mad."

Kitty thought about what Father Bauer had said to her in the confessional. "Go in peace and God bless you," said Kitty.

"No," said Eileen, patiently. "Let me be the priest and you tell me really bad sins."

The girls exchanged places and Kitty confessed sins as bad as Eileen had. She said a secret prayer in her mind to remind God that this was just play-acting, it was not a real confession. She hoped God heard her. With so many many people in the world to keep track of, Kitty thought it would be an easy mistake on God's (or anyone's) part to misunderstand, or misclassify. Kitty wondered if any sinners slipped into heaven by mistake, or vice versa — saints got sent to hell. Perhaps she and Eileen were playing with fire . . .

When Kitty said, "I am sorry for all of my sins," at the end of her imaginary confession, the "priest" began to shout at her: "You are going straight to hell! And for your penance, say two hundred Hail Marys and a hundred and two Our Fathers and give fifty dollars to the poor." Here Eileen burst through the blanket and said, "And twenty-five whiplashes too!" Eileen ran to get her pillow and began lashing Kitty over the head. Kitty grabbed the other pillow and the two girls chased each other around and around the room, under the bed and on top of it, in the closet and out. Kitty couldn't remember when she had had such a good time!

When they collapsed, laughing and exhausted, on Eileen's bed, Kitty said, "I didn't know Confession was so much fun to play."

"I know a lot of fun games," said Eileen.

Before dinner the girls went down into Eileen's basement where her father had put up a swing for her. Kitty had never seen a swing in a basement. She swung through the air so high that her feet touched the rafters of the ceiling. Then Eileen's father came home and picked

Eileen up and swung her in the air over his head saying, "How is my favorite girl tonight?" He had Fanny Farmer suckers in his pocket for both girls, and he wore his office suit to the table to eat dinner.

On the dinner table were candles in silver holders (lit) and napkins in napkin rings. The napkin rings matched the sterling silver knives and forks and spoons, and none of the food was anything Kitty recognized. Eileen told her it was just broccoli in cheese sauce, and "the same old" sole in wine sauce. After dessert (which was lemon mousse, Eileen said) the girls sat by the fire and looked at the magazines and books that were on the coffee table in the living room.

Then Eileen's father came in and asked if he could have the pleasure of "chauffeuring" Kitty home. The girls got ready and Eileen's father brought the car to the back door and opened the door for Kitty and Eileen to get in. As they drove along Albert Street, past the school huddled darkly for the night, Kitty felt the way Eileen must feel all the time: like a princess. In the high back seat of Eileen's sedan this was her special coach taking her directly home. Not like the streetcar, which carried everyone in the same general direction.

When they arrived at Kitty's house, Eileen's father got out and opened the door for her, took her arm, and walked her to her own front door. Kitty thanked him and waved to Eileen and went into her own house that seemed small now and a bit drab by comparison to Eileen's. Her mother sat darning socks in the living room and her father read the newspaper, but there was no warm fire and no sparkle of conversation.

Only after she was tucked safely into bed did she remember Father Bauer's sermon, and her quest for sainthood.

7

Saint Kitty

In the morning Kitty felt guilty for forgetting to be holy. It was confusing having two friends who were so different. She thought back over the good time she'd had at Eileen's house, and tried to remember if she had committed any sins. Surely saints did not play Confession. Or talk about priests and nuns. Margaret Mary did not play games with the sacraments. Instead, she helped her mother. Kitty wondered if Eileen ever helped her mother . . .

Kitty hurried off to mass and sat beside Margaret Mary, who was devoutly praying, counting off Our Fathers and Hail Marys on her crystal rosary beads.

At the sermon, Father Bauer told a sad story of a small boy who went to play baseball on Sunday morning instead of going to mass.

"On the way home," he said softly, "still carrying his bat and ball" (Father's voice grew dramatic here), "the lad crossed the street and was hit by a car. By the time they got him to the hospital, he was dead."

Kitty shuddered. She could not afford even momentary indiscretions. Margaret Mary did not look alarmed. But then, Margaret Mary did not sin.

Kitty was still shaking when they got to the playground. Margaret Mary slipped her daily missal into its case, after putting the satin ribbon between the pages of the next day's mass. She coiled her rosary into its silver box, like a snake in a basket, and slipped it into her uniform pocket. Eileen was waiting on the swing set, peeling an orange. She threw the peels over the schoolyard fence into the fields beyond Saint Anthony's. Margaret Mary looked for a moment as if she wanted to climb the fence and pick them up.

"I thought of some really good sins for Confession," Eileen said. "Next time we play."

"You *play* Confession?" said Margaret Mary. "Confession is a sacrament!"

Kitty was embarrassed. She felt like two people — one who was a saintly mass-goer and another who was a frivolous fun-seeker. It was very uncomfortable being with Eileen and Margaret Mary at the same time. She wasn't sure *who* she was.

"How can you go to mass every day, and then make fun of the sacraments?" Margaret Mary demanded.

"You go to mass every day?" said Eileen to Kitty in surprise. "You never told me that you like to pray!"

"Well, I do sometimes," said Kitty, trapped between her two friends. She had the awful feeling of being in the middle, and pulled on both sides. What did she really believe? Both Eileen and Margaret Mary knew exactly what they believed. They didn't hesitate or waver or act pulled two ways.

"I like to do different things with different people," said Kitty defensively.

"My mother says you can't serve both God and Mammon," said Margaret Mary. "You have to choose. Like the martyrs. They died for what they believed."

Kitty had no intention of dying for what she believed. She didn't even *know* what she believed.

Eileen had lost interest when the conversation turned to martyrs and had turned to Ruthie and a group of girls who were laughing at the other end of the playground. Kitty could see that Eileen and Margaret Mary would never be friends with each other. If they were together at all, it would be only because they were both friends of Kitty's. They seemed to dislike each other very much. Margaret Mary's face got red, and she looked angry whenever they met. And

Eileen, Kitty was sure, did not like to hear stories about what Margaret Mary's mother thought. At this rate, Kitty might lose both friends! Or perhaps Eileen would influence her to forget sainthood and just have fun! Kitty pictured Margaret Mary dashing in and plucking her away from temptation and Eileen, and maybe even saving her soul! It looked as if life at Saint Anthony's would be filled with excitement and challenge.

Before Margaret Mary could launch into another lecture about sainthood to her captive audience of one, the bell rang and the school day began.

Kitty worried all day that she'd fall into sin and go to hell. She also worried that she was always going to be in the middle, between her two new friends. Whenever the three of them were together, she would not be sure what she thought.

On the way home from school she avoided all the busy streets she could, and when she had to cross Jefferson she stood on the curb while everyone else ran across dodging traffic. She waited until there was no car in sight coming from any direction.

In her own house she carefully avoided walking near the basement steps — her mother's highly waxed floors were slippery, and Kitty was taking no chances of slipping and tumbling down to the cement below and getting a fatal blow to the head.

She considered calling Father Bauer at the rectory and asking him to hear her confession, but she did not know how he would feel about being disturbed during his supper when she was supposed to go to confession at regularly scheduled times, like three o'clock on Saturday afternoon. It was a long time till Saturday. She could slip on a banana peel or smother under her blanket on her bed, or even die of polio as two children in her class at Saint James had in first grade.

At bedtime, Kitty's mother ran her bath, but Kitty said she was not dirty enough to have a bath. "I can just wash," she said.

"Nonsense," said her mother. "Get into the tub and you will be much cleaner."

Kitty did not care about being cleaner. She cared more about the fact that she could fall asleep in the tub and slip into the water and drown. Father Bauer had not mentioned any little boys that had done that, but she was sure he had stories like that, and more, of children dying with sin on their souls and going to hell.

She washed in the washbowl, and let the water out of the tub quietly. Now she wondered about the fourth commandment; she had disobeyed her mother. Being Catholic at Saint Anthony's was becoming very very difficult. Sainthood was not nearly as easy as Father Bauer painted it.

By the time her father came in to tuck her in bed for the night she felt close to tears. "I'm going to hell," she cried out to him. "Everyone will be a saint but me!"

Kitty's father put his arm around her and listened to her story about Father Bauer's sermons, and the quest for sainthood, and how she had more fun with Eileen (a sinner) than with Margaret Mary (a saint).

He thought about it all for a while, and then he said, "You know, you can't go to hell accidentally."

Kitty wiped her nose with the hanky her father handed her.

"It isn't easy to be bad," he went on. "You can't be tricked."

"What if it's something awful, like" (Kitty wasn't ready to tell him about playing Confession) "missing mass on Sunday?"

"You have to say, 'I know this is a mortal sin, and I want to go to hell,'" her father said reassuringly.

"I *don't* want to go to hell," said Kitty.

"Then you won't," said her father. "I told you, you take life too seriously."

Kitty gave her father a kiss and a hug and he turned out the light. She had to *want* to go to hell! That is one thing Father Bauer never told her! What if that little boy who played baseball didn't even know about hell? He could be in heaven right now! It might just be possible, thought Kitty, that she would not have to work that hard to be a saint.

Worry made a person awfully tired, she thought. She turned over and fell asleep quickly.

8

The "B" Movie

Kitty felt much better going to school the next morning. Having solved the biggest problem, the other one did not loom so large. After all, what if she was in the middle? That may just be her nature. Her mother had once called one of her aunts "flexible," and it seemed like that was a good word for what she, Kitty, was. Sort of unpredictable. It could be something good; at least it wasn't boring. Kitty hated boring things.

After religion class, Sister Charlene told the class about something called the Legion of Decency pledge, which all Catholics took every year. Kitty knew about the Legion of Decency movie rating. Legion people went to all the movies that were made and looked for danger. They made a long list with harmless movies being rated "A," objectionable movies rated "B," and very sinful movies rated "C," for Condemned.

"Just remember to go only to 'A' movies." said Sister, "and you need not worry. 'B' movies could be sinful, and 'C' movies are a mortal sin without doubt."

Kitty's parents had the list hanging on the kitchen wall, and before Kitty went to a movie they looked at the rating. She had never seen a "B" movie. Kitty wondered if it was a sin for the Legion people to see the "B" and "C" movies. If not, she wondered if they enjoyed them. It might be fun to have the job of rating movies.

"Now it is time to take the Legion of Decency pledge," said Sister Charlene. "You raise your right hand, and repeat each line after me."

The class stood up and raised their right

hands. The pledge was long and the part about movies said, "I promise to stay away from 'B' and 'C' movies, and from movie theaters that show these movies . . ." The class mouthed the words after Sister, promising to go only to "A" movies. While they were repeating the words, Kitty looked at Eileen. Her hand was not up, and she was not saying the words. She was leaning on her desk, and appeared to be reading a library book.

At recess Kitty said, "Why didn't you say the words? We have to take that pledge, you know!"

"No, we don't," said Eileen, brushing her hair with the folding brush she carried in her pencil case. "No one is making me take any dumb pledge. My mom and dad don't believe in censorship anyway."

Kitty had no idea what censorship was, but she thought it must be something like citizenship — and surely it was wrong to not be a good citizen. However, Eileen did not seem to be a bit worried about it.

"Eileen, you can't go to 'B' movies!"

"I can go to any movie I want to," she said. "Swearing doesn't make a whole movie bad, you know."

Margaret Mary joined them in time to hear Eileen's statement. "You would go to a movie that had swear words in it?" she said with alarm.

"If it was a good movie," said Eileen.

Margaret Mary cast her eyes upward. Kitty thought perhaps she was saying a little prayer for Eileen.

"Well, Sunday there's a new movie at the Uptown, with Judy Garland and Mickey Rooney, and it's on the 'A' list," said Kitty.

The girls had been going to matinees together on Sundays. There were some good movies that were exciting enough for Eileen, but non-offensive to Margaret Mary like musicals and some of Walt Disney's.

"Judy Garland and Mickey Rooney are always safe," said Margaret Mary with satisfaction. "I'd like to go on Sunday."

"I would, too," said Kitty. "Are you coming, Eileen?"

Eileen shrugged. "I s'pose so," she said. "Judy Garland is boring, though."

"She is *wholesome*," said Margaret Mary. "My mother says we should patronize theaters that show wholesome movies."

Kitty liked Judy Garland. Ever since *The Wizard of Oz*, she had seen all of her movies.

"Let's meet at the corner of Randolph and Hamline," said Kitty. "At two o'clock."

Randolph and Hamline was out of the way for Kitty, but it was a midpoint for the girls to start the mile walk to the Uptown. They liked to walk together.

When Sunday came, Kitty arrived at the meeting place first. She had worn her lightweight tweed coat with the shiny buttons because it was her favorite coat, but as her mother had warned, the weather was too cold for it. Kitty jumped up and down to keep warm. Minnesota weather was erratic, her father said, and anytime after

October could chill you to the bone. Away in the distance, Kitty could see Eileen approaching. When she got closer Kitty could see that Eileen too was wearing her spring coat instead of a winter one.

Along with the lightweight coat, Eileen was wearing only knee socks. Kitty's mother made her wear long stockings (with the detested garter belt) during the school year.

"I'm freezing," said Eileen, rubbing her gloveless hands together to warm them. Her face was red, and both girls could see their breath in white clouds whenever they spoke.

"Let's go stand in the lobby of the Randolph till Margaret Mary comes," said Eileen, pulling Kitty along to the theater nearby.

The two girls looked at the billboards with the posters advertising the Randolph movie.

"Betty Grable!" said Eileen. "I'd rather see her any day, than Judy Garland."

Kitty looked doubtful.

"I think we should go to *this* movie instead of

the Uptown," Eileen went on. "I don't feel like walking a mile and freezing to death just to see Judy Garland."

Kitty saw Margaret Mary coming down the street and stepped out to hail her. "In here," she called.

Margaret Mary was bundled up in a heavy wool coat with a fur collar that her mother had cut down and made over from an adult coat. It looked very warm. She had long warm stockings on, and a wool cap her mother had knit, and matching woolen mittens. She did not look cold.

"We're going to the Uptown!" said Margaret Mary, with a glance at Betty Grable's legs.

"It's too far to the Uptown," said Eileen. "I'll freeze to death."

Margaret Mary looked disgusted. "That is because you don't have a winter coat on," she said. "My mother said the best way to get the flu is to get chilled."

Kitty had to admit Margaret Mary's mother was probably right. But it was provoking to have someone always do the right thing. It was fun wearing the tweed coat even if it was risky. Margaret Mary never did anything risky.

"Well, cold or not, I'm not going to a 'B' movie," said Margaret Mary. "Betty Grable is not an example of Christian womanhood, with her bare legs and . . . other things."

"She's a pin-up girl for the servicemen," said Eileen. "That is what pin-up girls do, show their bare legs! She has beautiful legs, like a dancer's." Eileen looked admiringly at the poster.

"We don't know it's a 'B' movie," urged Kitty.

"All movies with all that skin showing are 'B' movies," said Margaret Mary.

People bought their tickets and walked past them into the warm theater where they looked ready to see all the bare skin with no qualms. They carried popcorn and candy bars and did not seem to have Christian womanhood on their minds at all.

The girls studied the other posters. In one Betty Grable was draped in the arms of a dark-haired, mustached Latin lover, it appeared. Her blond hair flowed over his arm and down her back. She was barefoot.

"Well, I'm going in," said Eileen, marching over to the ticket window and putting her money down.

"Come on," urged Kitty, worried now that she would be in the lobby all day long with Margaret Mary. "We can see Judy Garland next Sunday. We're here now."

Margaret Mary hesitated.

"It probably isn't a 'B' movie," said Kitty. "I don't think they even show 'B' movies at this theater."

Kitty took the heavy sleeve of Margaret Mary's coat and led her toward the ticket window.

"I don't know . . ." Margaret Mary said reluctantly.

Kitty said, "Two, please," and finally Margaret Mary got her money out and paid for her ticket. The girls caught up with Eileen and got candy and popcorn and walked down the long carpeted aisle behind the usher, who carried a flashlight so they would not stumble.

They got three seats right in the middle and unbuttoned their coats, settling comfortably with their popcorn.

Before long the lights went out entirely, the curtain parted, and the newsreel came on the screen. THE EYES AND THE EARS OF THE WORLD! said large letters on the flickering screen. Then tanks rolled by and planes overhead opened the bomb-bay doors and rained bombs on the enemy.

The newsreel went on to show fighting in the trenches and in the hedgerows in Europe. Then there was a film showing all of the children being evacuated from London in trucks to the country. The girls chewed their popcorn thoughtfully. Kitty and Margaret Mary said silent prayers for the children and, as Sister Charlene had told them to, for all the dying soldiers who fought for peace.

"We are going to be in the war soon, my dad says," said Eileen.

The thought alarmed Kitty. Between Margaret Mary's mother and Eileen's father, she was alarmed a good deal of the time.

When the battle scenes came on and showed "the Allies steadily advancing," the audience cheered and whistled. When the screen showed Hitler, they all booed loudly.

After the newsreel, a "short" came on the screen called "What You Don't Eat," which showed how sailors (and some civilians) got scurvy and beriberi and rickets from not drinking milk and eating oranges and grains. It was almost as alarming as the newsreel. But then Donald Duck came on and another Looney Tune, and the audience was able to forget the grim part of life and laugh when Donald and his three nephews fell overboard in a rowboat.

By the time the movie started, the girls were in good spirits. But it was not long before Kitty knew they were in trouble.

Betty Grable appeared to be friends with many servicemen in the movie and spent a good deal of time kissing them good-bye as they left for war. She kissed them again when they came home on furloughs, and in between she kissed men who were 4-F and could not go to war at all.

"I think this is a 'B' movie," whispered Margaret Mary to Kitty, very early in the movie.

"It is too early to tell," lied Kitty.

Eileen took no notice of the problem and was settled back in her seat with her feet up on the seat in front of her. She was popping gumdrops into her mouth, and her eyes were glued to the screen.

Now Betty was dancing for the troops, and taking off some of her clothes (a scarf, a stocking) and throwing it into the audience. The audience scrambled for the articles, and Betty sang and danced on.

Margaret Mary fidgeted in the seat next to Kitty. It made Kitty more nervous than she already was.

The dance was over, and Betty was in a taxicab. The man next to her was saying, "You are a darn swell dame."

Margaret Mary was almost on her feet now.

"That is *swearing*!" she said. "Swearing means a 'B' movie!"

"*Darn* is not swearing," said Eileen from her seat on the other side of Kitty. "*Damn* is swearing."

The two girls looked at Eileen. Eileen actually said a swear word! The movie was a bad influence on Eileen!

Kitty worried about how much worse the movie could get. What if Betty took off all of her clothes? Then it would be a 'C' movie, instead of a 'B'. What if someone said "damn" instead of "darn," next? Kitty quivered. She had to admit she was enjoying it. They were here, she may as well. Kitty wondered why it was so much more fun to do something risky than something that they knew was all right. Why was this movie so much more fun to see than Judy Garland would be? Was she really a sinner? Did she, deep down, like wicked things better than good things?

"I love you so," the dark Latin Lover was whispering into Betty's ear.

"But I have a husband," pleaded Betty, caressing his neck.

Before Betty could say another word, Margaret Mary stood up, her popcorn spraying in all directions.

"We have to leave!" she said, gathering her coat and belongings together. "She is a married woman with boyfriends!"

Kitty pulled at her sleeve. "Sit down," she whispered. "Everyone is looking at us."

They were. All heads were turned toward Margaret Mary.

"This is a 'B' movie!" said Margaret Mary loudly, for all to hear. "No one should be here."

Kitty felt her face turn red in the dark. Eileen did not pay any attention. Her eyes were on the screen.

"We have to leave!" Margaret Mary stamped her foot. "Put your coats on."

"I'm not leaving," said Eileen.

"Kitty? Get your coat on. This is a 'B' movie."

Kitty wished Margaret Mary would sit down and be quiet. She couldn't imagine anything worse than crawling over everyone in their row, all eyes on them, as they left the theater. She'd rather die.

"Sit down!" shouted someone who was behind Margaret Mary and could not see.

Margaret Mary did not sit down. Instead she said, "I am going to talk to the manager of this theater about showing bad movies."

People were beginning to boo Margaret Mary! They had paid their money, and they wanted to see the movie. Kitty wanted to slide onto the floor and be invisible under the seats.

"You are embarrassing us," said Kitty.

"Is it embarrassing to do what's right?" she said. "Father Bauer said it isn't easy to be a Christian. That's the price we have to pay for sainthood!"

Kitty wondered why she ever was Margaret Mary's friend. Rather than let this go on and on, she put her coat over her head and followed Margaret Mary down the aisle, just as the usher was coming to see what the noise was all about.

Kitty went to the rest room while Margaret

Mary went to the manager's office. She felt angry about missing the rest of the movie. There was Eileen, enjoying it to the end. Why couldn't Kitty stand up for her rights? Why was she so weak?

The manager was not in, and Margaret Mary and Kitty sat in the lounge in the lobby and waited for the movie to be out so that Eileen could join them. Margaret Mary's face was red. She looked very angry. Kitty thought Eileen would look guilty and sheepish when she came out, but instead she had tears of joy in her eyes.

"That was so good," she said. "David went into battle and was killed in the end — it was so sad. What a good movie!"

"Is David the dark guy?" said Kitty.

"Yeah," said Eileen. "He is the one she liked the best."

On the way home, Eileen and Kitty talked about the movie. Margaret Mary walked ahead of them, alone. At the corner, she announced, "I am stopping in at the rectory to go to confession. I don't want a mortal sin on my soul overnight."

"That's dumb," said Eileen.

"It's almost suppertime," Kitty added. "Father Bauer will be eating supper."

"This is more important than any supper," said Margaret Mary. "And it isn't dumb to get rid of a sin."

She turned the corner by the church, and the girls waved. At the next corner Kitty waved good-bye to Eileen and walked toward Jefferson Avenue.

When she got into the house, the first thing she did (after wiping her feet) was to look at the Legion of Decency list. She found the Betty Grable movie listed.

It was on the "A" list.

9

The Lay Teacher

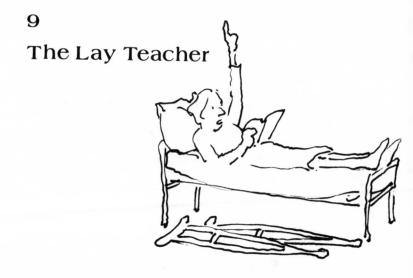

The next week, Kitty's uniform came, all blue and stiff and clean. She put it on, and when she got to school she blended in with the other students. Even though she had her uniform and new friends and did not feel as strange as she had at first, little things kept coming up that kept her "the new girl." Things that she did not know — things that Saint James had not taught. She was not quite at home yet.

One of the things came up a few weeks later. Winter was settling in in Saint Paul, and the students at Saint Anthony's were bundling up in teddy bear coats and warm parka hoods. Sister

Charlene had to allow them more time for getting out of wraps and getting back into them, at recess and dismissal. Kitty wondered how the nuns kept warm — they always appeared to wear the same thing, long, black serge habits with the veil, in any temperature, winter or summer. Perhaps, she thought, they added and subtracted underwear to fit the season.

One morning, after all of the boots and mittens and scarves had been put into the cloakroom and everyone was seated, rosy-cheeked and ready for prayer and the flag salute, Sister Charlene said she had some news.

The class sat in their "news" position — feet on the floor and hands folded on the desks. Sister looked a little bit embarrassed.

"Boys and girls," she began. "I shall have to be away next month — it may be a week or two before I am back at Saint Anthony's."

Sister Charlene had everyone's interest. Even Eileen looked up in surprise. Nuns did not go away, or take vacations, or get sick. What could she possibly have to go away for? Kitty grew excited, hoping Sister would say, "There will be no school for the third grade during those weeks." Margaret Mary looked worried.

"Of course I shall hurry back just as fast as I can," Sister went on. "I don't like disrupting our routine and losing precious learning time."

Kitty thought privately that was just exactly what *she* did like — a welcome change from what had become a sort of boring school day. Sister's leaving would be a change, no matter what happened.

"I would not leave unless it was absolutely necessary — this is something absolutely imperative that I must attend to," Sister said.

"I wonder what it is," whispered Eileen.

"I shall miss every one of you very much of course, and I will trust you all to carry on the same as if I was here."

Then they did have to come to school — there was to be no vacation for the third grade. Would they be alone? Unsupervised? On their honor?

"While I am gone," said Sister Charlene, "and since we are short-staffed, you will be taught by a lay teacher." Knowing looks appeared on some faces, and sounds of "oh" and "ah" filled the air. Kitty had no idea what a lay teacher was. Everyone else in the room seemed to know, except her.

"Although she is a lay teacher," Sister was saying, "I will expect you all to treat her with the same respect and obedience that you give me — or Sister Justina." Sister made the lay teacher sound just a bit inferior, perhaps not quite deserving of the same loyalty, Kitty thought. Otherwise, why would she have suggested it be any different?

"I shall leave lesson plans and the schedule and your worksheets here, so that you can go ahead with your work just as if I were here. The lay teacher will find everything ready for her."

Now she made lay teachers sound not quite as smart as regular teachers, thought Kitty. People needing things ready for them, as if they would bumble if they proceeded on their own. Perhaps lay teachers were unfinished — teachers whom the school hired at bargain prices because of some flaw. "Lay" may mean inferior!

"Now we will go on with our work. I wanted to tell you ahead of time, so that you will be ready when the time comes."

What in the world could Kitty do to get ready for a lay teacher? Everyone else probably knew, and she would be the only one unprepared! Kitty made up her mind that she would not let anyone know that she did not know what a lay teacher was. It would mark her more than ever the "new girl," just when she was beginning to fit in.

There was much discussion about the lay teacher at recess time.

"We had a lay teacher once in kindergarten," said Eileen, drawing in the dirt with a stick on the playground. "She was always late, and she kind of lisped." Eileen imitated the lay teacher and everyone laughed.

"I don't think it's right to laugh at lay teachers," said Margaret Mary.

Then lay teachers *were* inferior. They were late and couldn't talk right and people laughed at them. Kitty felt a surge of pity for these poor creatures. She made up her mind that she would be particularly nice to her — go out of her way to be respectful. Kitty wondered where these lay teachers came from. Was there a home for them? An institution where someone looked after them?

All day Kitty wondered about them. That night, at the dinner table, Kitty said, "Guess what?"

Her mother and father couldn't guess.

"Sister Charlene is going away and we are going to have a lay teacher to teach us."

Kitty watched the look on her parents' faces for any evidence of explanation.

"They deserve work too," said her father, passing Kitty the mashed potatoes. "Although I wouldn't want you to have one on a full-time basis, as they do in some of the Catholic schools in Minneapolis."

"I don't know," said Kitty's mother. "That is why we are sending you to a Catholic school — to be taught by nuns. I don't think it is quite fair to bring in lay teachers."

Then a lay teacher was not a nun! Kitty tried to picture what one would look like. Not only lisping and late and inferior, but this person would even look different physically!

Kitty began to fear this unknown being. That night she dreamed that everyone in the third grade understood the lay teacher but her. Instead of English, when she spoke to Kitty, the words came out in French or Greek and were just a hodgepodge of sounds Kitty didn't understand, so she could not obey even the simplest commands. Kitty woke up sweating and nervous.

Every day in school Sister Charlene talked about the lay teacher.

"Remember, the lay teacher won't know your names for a while," she said one day. "Maybe we should make name tags to help her."

"Margaret Mary, while the lay teacher is here, perhaps you can call the ranks since she does not know the patrol boys or the streets," she said another day.

"Yes, Sister," said Margaret Mary, who seemed confident she could cope.

"Sister Justina will come into our room for religion class while I'm gone," said Sister Charlene another day. "The lay teacher is Lutheran, so she cannot teach religion, of course. But be sure to be a fine example of Catholicism for her. Remember, the best way to win a convert is by good example."

Lutheran! On top of every thing else, the lay teacher was Lutheran! Kitty could not wait to race home and announce this development to her parents.

"Why would they hire a Lutheran lay teacher?" said Kitty's mother at dinner.

"At the meeting of the Men's Club, they said they were not able to get a Catholic lay teacher," said Kitty's father. "There is a real teacher shortage in town."

"Do you mean all lay teachers are not Lutheran?" said Kitty.

"Of course not," said her mother. "Why would they all be Lutheran?"

Kitty excused herself and went to her room. She got down her dictionary and decided to look up "lay teacher." There had to be a definition — and Sister Charlene and her father both encouraged her to use the dictionary when she wanted to know the meaning of something.

Kitty paged through the dictionary, but there was no "lay teacher" listed. Her finger fell on the word *lay*, and she read, "To put in a horizontal or reclining position."

Of course. She had known that all the time. *Lay* was a simple word. If you put it in front of *teacher*, it must mean a teacher who reclined, who was horizontal. They may not all be Lutheran, but they all must recline! Why would a teacher recline? She must have been in an accident and be crippled, Kitty decided. Perhaps she would arrive on a stretcher, or at least on crutches. No wonder this teacher needed things prepared for her!

It surely would not be easy to manage a third grade class of boys and girls from a horizontal position! Kitty wondered if Sister Justina would bring in the cot from the nurse's office for the lay teacher.

Kitty felt more confidence on the playground now, knowing as much as the other people about lay teachers.

"I wonder where old Charlene is going?" said Eileen, one day. Eileen often referred to the nuns without saying Sister, which was disrespectful, Margaret Mary said.

"I know I want to be all the help I can to the lay teacher," said Margaret Mary.

"She will sure need it," agreed Kitty. "I wonder how she'll get here?"

"On the streetcar, like anyone who doesn't live in the neighborhood," said Eileen.

"Or a taxicab," said Margaret Mary.

"They don't earn enough for taxicabs," said Eileen.

The more Kitty heard, the sorrier she felt for lay teachers! Crippled, reclining, lisping probably, Lutheran, and yet having to go out to work every day! It didn't seem fair. And to come on the streetcar! An ambulance would be a better way. Kitty said a prayer for the lay teacher under her breath. She had never prayed for a Lutheran before. But surely they deserved prayers as much as any healthy Catholic.

A few days before Sister Charlene was to leave, she said to the class, "It would be a good idea to welcome the lay teacher with some small gift. She will feel like an outsider at first, and a small bouquet of flowers or a fruit basket would be a nice token of respect."

At recess the whole third grade was agog with talk of what to bring the lay teacher.

"I might bring her a scapular," said Margaret Mary.

"She isn't even Catholic. What would she do with it?" asked Eileen.

"She could still wear it," said Margaret Mary. "It would bring her grace and maybe convert her some day."

Eileen looked disgusted. "She probably likes being Lutheran just fine. I'm going to bring her some cookies. My mom makes real good coconut cookies."

Kitty did not say what she was going to bring

the lay teacher. When she got home after school, she asked her mother for some white material from her sewing basket. Then she found some white thread and a needle and went to her room and shut the door. She had a good idea for something the lay teacher was bound to like. It was something that she surely could use. If she lay on the small cot from the nurse's office, it would be difficult to see the class. Kitty would make her a pillow so that her head would be higher, and she could see everyone better.

She took an old pillow from a discarded doll's bed (she had not played with her dolls all year, with new Saint Anthony things on her mind) and measured it for a clean new cover. On the cover she would embroider something pretty to cheer the lay teacher up and help her forget about her misfortune.

All afternoon and evening Kitty cut and sewed the pillowcase. When it was finished, it fit just right and felt nice and soft. She found some colored embroidery thread and embroidered some roses in one corner. They turned out to look more like small balloons, but they were colorful and gay. The one corner took so long that she decided she would only do two corners altogether. There was one more day before the lay teacher arrived. She would do the other corner tomorrow.

"What are you bringing for the lay teacher?" asked Margaret Mary, the next morning.

"It's a surprise," said Kitty. "I made it myself." Kitty did not want to talk about her gift. She felt it was sort of personal.

In the classroom, the little table beside Sister Charlene's desk was beginning to fill up with small packages. There were two apples and an orange, and a very small package from Margaret Mary (Kitty guessed it was the scapular), and the box of cookies from Eileen.

Margaret Mary had cut neat letters out of colored paper, saying "Good-bye, Sister Charlene, and God Bless You," and put them on the bulletin board in the front of the room. The time had come for her to leave. The next morning the poor crippled lay teacher would arrive.

At home that night, Kitty finished embroidering the pillow. In another corner she sewed "L.T. from Kitty." She found "lay teacher" too long to embroider, and she was almost out of blue thread. She wrapped the pillow carefully in the white tissue paper from one of her birthday presents and tied it with white string from the bakery. It just fit into her plaid school bag, so she was able to leave in the morning with no questions from her mother.

The children were excited at school. When the bell rang on the playground, there was no Sister Charlene to meet them and see that the line was straight. Margaret Mary stood in the front of the line and took her place, giving, Kitty noticed, the same nod and look of firmness that Sister had. Margaret Mary would be a very good nun, thought Kitty. It would be just the right vocation for her.

When they got to the room, no one was there.

No cot was set up — no crutches leaned against the wall. As Kitty put her gift on the table with the others, she noticed it was by far the largest.

"What *is* that?" Eileen asked, frowning. "It looks like something to wear."

"It isn't," said Kitty.

The class sat at their desks with their hands folded, when suddenly Sister Justina hurried in.

"Boys and girls," she said, "Mrs. Freeman will be here very soon. Meanwhile, you go on with things just as if she were already here."

So the lay teacher had a name! She was a Mrs. — Mrs. Freeman. Sister Justina bustled out, and Margaret Mary asked the class to stand for prayer and the flag salute. After that, everyone sat down and looked at the door expectantly.

"We should take out our library books," announced Margaret Mary, "so that she will see that we are working."

Everyone took out a library book, except a boy named Robert, who began to shoot rubber bands around the room. Kitty wondered if the ambulance men would be able to hold the door open and get the stretcher and bed in all alone. She thought of reminding Margaret Mary of the problem and perhaps volunteering some help. Kitty could not help but note that Eileen had been right, lay teachers were late. But of course they had a very good reason for being late. Crippled people could not get around very easily. They surely could not run to catch a streetcar, or hurry if they found themselves behind schedule.

All of a sudden the classroom door burst open, and a very young woman with blond hair and rosy cheeks rushed in, carrying an armful of books. She must be Mrs. Freeman's nurse, thought Kitty. But instead of helping someone else in through the door, the blond girl pulled the door closed after her, went over to Sister Charlene's desk, dumped her books there in a heap, and ran a comb that she had taken from her coat pocket through her hair. She tossed her coat over a nearby chair, and walked down to face the class. Then she smiled. A very big, healthy smile.

And standing very firmly on her own two very uncrippled legs, she said, "Hi! My name is Mrs. Freeman, and I am going to be your teacher for the next couple of weeks!"

10

The New Girl in Third Grade

Kitty had the feeling that she had somehow been tricked. Even the dictionary was not reliable. Here was the lay teacher before her, not crippled, not reclining — not even lisping! She was not only very healthy, but she was a normal person. A person one might meet on the street, wearing normal clothes, un-nunlike, no doubt eating normal food, and living in a normal house — not an institution. Why, if Kitty met her on the street, she would have no single way of identifying this person as a lay teacher at all!

Part of Kitty felt relieved — it would be exciting to have a teacher just like the public school children had. The other part of her felt a loss for the person she had developed in her mind — the invalid who would need her help. She wondered how she had ever become so sure of what the lay teacher would be like. No doubt her parents were right when they reminded Kitty that she had a wild imagination. Her father said she tended to exaggerate a story when she told it. She even exaggerated stories that were in her mind, she decided. She would have to stop that. It always seemed to get her in some kind of trouble.

Mrs. Freeman had hung her coat up now, and Margaret Mary was explaining the daily schedule. Mrs. Freeman looked puzzled. No doubt she had not been in a Catholic school before.

"How nice you all look, all in blue!" she said. "And what well-behaved children you are!"

She must be used to children like the ones at Randolph Heights, the neighboring public school, where (Kitty heard) no one stayed at his desk, but they all ran through the halls and came in from the playground without lining up at all.

"Thank you, Mrs. Freeman," said the class in unison.

Mrs. Freeman giggled. She must think good manners are funny, thought Kitty.

She walked over to the small table where the gifts were. That gave Kitty a brand-new problem: What in the world would she think of someone giving her a pillow? And what would the whole class think? It would just confirm the fact Kitty did not fit in. She was a new girl still.

Maybe Mrs. Freeman would take the gifts home! Of course that was what she'd do! She would not take precious school time to open them.

"Why how generous of you all," said Mrs. Freeman when she was told the gifts were for her. She drew the desk chair up to the little table and began to unwrap the first tissue-covered package.

Kitty felt her face get pink already. She *was* going to open the things in front of everyone. Kitty wanted to leave. She wanted to disappear. She wished she'd stayed home sick in bed.

"A handkerchief!" Mrs. Freeman was saying.

"And how pretty it is!" She tucked the hanky into the pocket of her ruffly white blouse.

She began opening more gifts and exclaiming over them. She said nice things about the fruit and the flowers and made the class feel very happy about their choices.

But what could she possibly say about a *pillow?* She would act surprised no doubt and say, "Why do I need this?" and Kitty would grow red and embarrassed and everyone would know she was the one that had chosen such an inappropriate gift. They would point again, and laugh, and on the playground they would still be whispering about it at recess.

Finally Kitty's large box was the only one left.

"The mystery box," said Mrs. Freeman, tearing off the tissue paper. "What could this possibly be?"

Kitty closed her eyes. She could not watch Mrs. Freeman's face.

"Why," said Mrs. Freeman's voice, "what an appropriate gift! Kitty?" she asked. "Which one of you is Kitty?"

Kitty raised her hand without opening her eyes.

"Why Kitty, how did you know we had a baby at home to use this?" she said. "I'll bet Sister Charlene told you! And did you embroider this all by yourself?"

Kitty nodded her head. She couldn't believe her ears! Mrs. Freeman *liked* her gift! Mrs. Freeman had a *baby!* She did not look old enough to be married and have a baby!

"Well, it was very thoughtful. I saved the best for last."

The best! Mrs. Freeman actually liked hers the best! Lay teachers were just one surprise after the other! There was just no predicting what could happen with them.

On the playground at recess, people circled around Kitty.

"How did you know she had a baby?" demanded Eileen.

"She liked yours *best*," said Margaret Mary. "I thought my scapular was pretty nice, but she didn't say anything."

"She probably didn't know what it was." Eileen laughed.

After recess Mrs. Freeman asked Kitty to help her put the gifts into a box, so she could get them ready to carry home. Kitty felt a flood of warmth toward this teacher who understood her. She wished Sister Charlene would never come back. She wished the class could have a lay teacher forever!

At suppertime, Kitty was bursting with stories to tell. "The lay teacher likes me," she boasted while her mother served the pork chops. "She likes our whole class. She says we are the best-mannered class she has ever taught."

Her mother and father listened politely. "She has a baby," Kitty went on. "And she wears very pretty clothes."

"I just hope she knows her job," said Kitty's mother.

Kitty told them all she learned in arithmetic. "And in phonics," she went on, taking another pork chop, "she told us a rhyme to remember. 'When two vowels go walking, the first one does the talking.' As in *rain* or *beat*. Sister Charlene never told us things like that."

When Kitty was ready for bed, and her father was tucking her in, Kitty said (without fear now), "Why do they call them lay teachers?"

"Perhaps we should look it up in the dictionary," said her father.

"I already did," said Kitty. "*Lay* means to recline — and that would be silly, for a teacher . . ." Kitty laughed nervously.

"You were looking at the wrong *lay*. That *lay* is a verb. There is another *lay* farther down that is an adjective. The adjective means 'secular,' which means 'not belonging to a religious order.' A lay teacher is someone who is not a nun."

So the dictionary was reliable after all! Kitty was relieved that it had not let her down. She just had not read far enough. She would have to remember not to stop after the first definition of a word.

The days with the lay teacher passed quickly. One day Mrs. Freeman had Kitty show some of the girls how to embroider. Sister Charlene would never have let them sew in class. A lay teacher was just what a Catholic school needed, thought Kitty. It was a happy two weeks. One afternoon Mrs. Freeman even brought her baby to school, and Kitty took care of it during recess. A real baby in the classroom!

The whole class was sorry to see Mrs. Freeman leave, and when Sister Charlene returned and said, "I hope the adjustment to a lay teacher was not too hard on you," they all were thinking (but not saying), "I wish she could have stayed longer."

First communion day came and went for the third grade. Kitty had a lot of time to read library books, and on Holy Thursday she went to church to watch the class in their white suits and dresses and veils, even though she had made her own first communion a year earlier.

The winter in Saint Paul was cold and windy, and when Eileen or Margaret Mary came to Kitty's house after school, Kitty would bundle up warmly and walk them halfway home with her scarf stiff with frost from her warm breath. The afternoons were very short, and it grew dark and the streetlights came on before the girls had finished playing. They all looked forward to summer when school would be out, and they would have all day long — and long, long days — to play together.

One day almost at the end of winter, but before it was really spring, Kitty got to school just a moment after the bell on the playground had rung. There had been rubbery ice with water under it along the curb, and she had taken longer than she'd realized stepping on it and watching the water ooze up over the top. It was the kind of day when she itched to wear anklets and oxfords to school, without her snow boots, but her mother said, "This is just the weather to get your feet wet and catch a cold."

Kitty ran the last block, and when she arrived the lines had gone in already, but there inside the door stood a girl who looked as if she was about Kitty's own age, and she did not look familiar.

"Could you tell me where the third grade is?" she asked nervously, in a voice that sounded as though she might cry at any moment.

"Do you know which third grade?" asked Kitty.

The girl shook her head.

"I'll take you to the office," said Kitty. "Sister Justina will know what room you want."

On the way to the office, Kitty said, "Are you new here?"

The girl nodded. "We're from Chicago," she said. "We just moved here."

Feeling very knowledgeable, Kitty knocked bravely on the office door and told Sister Justina that there was a new girl for third grade (and it wasn't Kitty!).

"Why, we've been looking for you!" Sister said. "You must be Betty!"

Betty looked relieved that someone knew her name and was expecting her, and she thanked Kitty for helping her.

"Thank you, Kitty. You may go to your room

now and I will bring Betty up later," said Sister Justina.

The halls were quiet now, with all of the students in their rooms and the doors shut. A last minute patrol boy put his sign in the hall rack and clambered away to his room.

Kitty stood a minute in the middle of the wide hall on the shiny tiled floor. She felt the silence around her in this huge, empty place, and she sniffed the smell of school. It smelled faintly of paper and books and chalk dust and disinfectant, and a little like shavings from lead pencils. Then the odor of apples too long in a lunch box wafted in with the others.

She remembered being here all alone, and very afraid, just a few short months ago. Now she was confident and knew exactly where to go, and people expected her to be here.

Suddenly she missed the terror of that first day. She tried to bring back the fear that had gripped her — she tried to pretend that she was new again and did not know where she was going.

She pretended to dash from door to door, trying to remember, to bring it back. Up the broad stairs — up, up, to a room of complete strangers at the top of the steps. She would go in — they would stare — she would want to run, down the stairs and out the door.

Kitty gave a shudder. It all came back now, the aloneness, the not belonging, the no one caring. She shook herself. She was imagining again! She was deep into another game of pretend. It could be dangerous, she knew, but it was so much fun! It was fun because it was not real! She came back quickly to the present and knew that she was not afraid anymore, she wasn't alone, and everyone inside that door knew her!

Kitty went in and told Sister Charlene she had taken a new girl to the office. Sister nodded, and Kitty took her seat. In a moment there was a knock on the door, and Sister Justina brought in the new girl and introduced her to the class. "Boys and girls," Sister said, "this is Betty, a new third grader, whom I hope you will make very welcome here at Saint Anthony's. She is all the way from Chicago."

Except for the part about Chicago, it could have been Kitty that Sister Justina was introducing! Kitty wondered if she said the same thing about everyone — she was not special after all! Well, there were only so many things you could say about a new girl, she thought.

Sister Charlene bustled about getting books for Betty and then said, "Kitty, could you make room for Betty to sit with you for the morning? Tomorrow she will have a desk of her own."

Sister was asking her, Kitty, to help the new girl! So Kitty really wasn't the new girl anymore! She belonged at Saint Anthony's right here in the classroom. And Betty looked as terrified as Kitty had a few months ago.

Kitty moved over to make room for Betty, and showed her where they were in their textbooks, just as Margaret Mary had shown her. Betty listened attentively, but she looked embarrassed. She wore a bright yellow sweater over her brown skirt, and she stood out in the crowd. She was different. And everyone turned around to look at her.

At recess Kitty introduced her to Eileen and Margaret Mary, and Margaret Mary asked Betty to go to church with her in the morning. Kitty felt relief at the thought that Margaret Mary might have someone new to make into a saint and to take to mass each morning.

Betty's coming seemed to be a sort of landmark for Kitty, the end of the old and beginning of the new. As she pictured Betty meeting Margaret Mary on the corner for a cold early walk to church, she wondered how *she* would handle differences — would she turn out to be dangerous, like Eileen — or holy, like Margaret Mary — or would she also be in the middle?

After school Kitty said, "See you tomorrow," to Betty. Then she and Eileen and Margaret Mary stayed after school to wash blackboards and clap the erasers against the bricks outside the building. Kitty watched Eileen and Margaret Mary laughing at something as they filled a pail of water and carried it together down the hall. She was the reason they got along! Her coming to Saint Anthony's had made a difference! They were still completely different, and yet here they were sharing a joke.

When they finished their work, Sister Charlene gave them candy bars and a holy card, and the three of them sat on the school steps eating and talking and laughing. It was good to have friends.

That evening Kitty curled up in her bed with a warm feeling. Suddenly she remembered something that Sister John Bosco had said, "The Lord works in strange ways . . ." and "Everything works together for the good of the Lord."

Well, it had. Everything had turned out just the way Sister had said it would.

How did nuns know so much, anyway?